BALLROOM BLIND DATE

LEWIS DANCESPORT NOVELLA

BALLROOM BLITZ EXTRAS
BOOK 1.5

NATALIE CROSS

PREFACE

Thank you so much for reading!

If you like this book, you can buy Ballroom Blitz wherever books are sold.

Please leave a review on your preferred site! It really helps.

1

The restaurant was too loud, an eclectic mix of too many different styles and genres, as if it couldn't decide which flash-in-the-pan viral trend it wanted to follow. The tables and chairs were industrial steel, uncomfortable, and unable to retain heat, despite the warm late spring evening. The enormous glass skylights just meant that the acoustics were completely off. To hear her order, the waiter had to lean barely an inch away from her face. His breath smelled like pancake syrup. Not that there was anyone for Tabitha to complain to—her supposed date was twenty minutes late.

Tabitha Valby sighed and sipped at her glass of viognier. So far, this restaurant's only redeeming feature was its wine-by-the-glass list.

Across the restaurant, she saw a couple, each dressed in high fashion, completely ignoring one other while posing for selfies every four minutes. Even that was preferable to being stood up at the age of forty-four.

She was too old for this, but she had promised her

friend and dance instructor Anita that she would meet Dennis. Tabitha always kept her promises.

She glanced at the half-full glass of wine. She couldn't drink like she used to, certainly not since she had turned forty. It would be better to savor it, even if he didn't show up.

She flicked her gaze around the restaurant again. No sign of Dennis No-Last-Name.

Fine. She didn't need him. She could easily entertain herself. She opened her phone screen, selected the House-Helper App, and as soon as its cheery white picket fence and blue-sky logo appeared, her shoulders relaxed, dropping an inch.

This was definitely her happy place. She opened her favorite search, three-bedroom homes in Lewis, Pennsylvania with fireplace, preferably with A/C for the humid summers.

She inhaled deeply, the oxygen filling her lungs and relaxing her muscles. A warm smile spread from her toes toward the crown of her curly brown hair. There it was.

Her dream house.

A gray and navy-blue Cape Cod set on half an acre, with a backyard large enough for a vegetable patch and a shade tree. A flat driveway that wouldn't be a beast to shovel on her own in the winter. The location was ideal, too, within walking distance of the train and easy access to the trails through the forests surrounding the town of Lewis. She could take her hypothetical dog for hypothetical long walks while listening to podcasts, like she had always dreamed of doing. It was a tad near the top end of her price range, but since the bathrooms needed some serious non-big box store renovation, she knew she could bid lower.

Who needed a non-existent man to share such a gem? It could be all hers. It would be all hers.

She refreshed the listing again, as she had done at least 372 times already that day. It had been on the market for three days so far, likely no offers yet. They had only posted the open house two hours ago, so there was a good chance no one else would be there. It was a tad peculiar, the last-minute nature of the open house, but real estate was a volatile industry. Hopefully there wouldn't be a ton of competition, so her offer would stand out, all pretty and gift-wrapped.

The second good thing about this restaurant, besides its wine-by-the-glass list, was its proximity to her future dream home. She could be there in ten minutes, have a walk through, and see if it lived up to its photogenic promise.

Screw late-ass Dennis.

Tabitha finished her wine, called for the check, and headed out the door of the too-loud, too-trendy restaurant.

2

Dennis Rayner adjusted the wire-frame spectacles on his nose and frowned. "I don't know about this wainscoting. Does wainscoting really sell any more?"

The real estate agent's smile looked pained. It would certainly hurt Dennis's face, if he were to attempt such an expression. "I don't know. This house has so many positives, I doubt it's a deal breaker for anyone." She checked her watch, pointedly. "Are you going to be much longer?"

He assumed she would have more patience if her open house had been a bigger success. He had already been there, admiring the gray and navy-blue Cape Cod, for the past twenty minutes, and no one else had arrived. If she wanted more of a turn out, the realtor ought to have posted it more than two hours ago, but he was not about to look this gift horse in the mouth.

He needed a deal on a place. Ever since Cynthia had called off their wedding, he had been living in a dreary one-bedroom with a leaky faucet and a landlord who blocked his calls.

"Hmm." Dennis checked his watch as well. He had a niggling sensation that he was forgetting something, but he couldn't remember. He did have a terrible memory for appointments.

He walked up the staircase to investigate the second story again. It was good to have all the bedrooms on one floor, but as he got older, he couldn't help but wonder about having at least one room on the ground floor. If it was going to be a forever home, he didn't want to be stumbling down stairs in his seventies. People broke hips that way, or worse. Maybe three bedrooms was too large. Cynthia had been his first real girlfriend, and he had been forty when he had met her. It wasn't likely he was going to fill all these bedrooms.

Though if he were, they would need to be repainted. Forest green and tan? This wasn't a hunting lodge.

His phone buzzed in his pocket as he inspected one of the bathrooms. He opened the under-sink cabinet. No mold, but the plywood had swollen and the entire set would need to be replaced. His pulse beat rapidly in his chest, the same thrill of conquest he always felt whenever he found a rare coin for his collection. This house was perfect. And if the attendance at the open house was any indication, he would actually be able to afford it, despite the costs incurred by his canceled wedding.

His phone buzzed again and he absentmindedly took it out of his pocket as he inspected the windowsill in the bathroom. It would need to be weather-proofed for the winter. Nothing a quick trip to the big box store couldn't fix.

It was a text from Anita Goodman, his dance instructor at Lewis Dancesport.

How's it going?

· · ·

Dennis wrinkled his nose and contemplated the message again. Anita was wonderful, really she was. After Cynthia had ditched him and the dance lessons she had insisted upon (and he had paid for), Anita had tried to help him come out of his shell and meet new people.

Wait. Meet new people.

Shit.

Dennis shoved the phone into his pocket and headed for the stairs. Maybe he wasn't *too* late. Why hadn't he started keeping appointment reminders like Cynthia had pleaded with him to do? How was it that he ran his own successful accounting firm and yet could not remember simple appointments? He needed a better assistant. If he could only get through the interviews, but it was so difficult connecting to people in such a short time.

He checked the clock on his phone, forcing his breathing to slow. He wouldn't be too late. The restaurant wasn't far from the house. He just had to hurry. And apologize profusely, with flowers or a charcuterie board or...something.

He rushed down the staircase, not even pausing to admire the wrought iron banister. As he reached the first floor, the front door swung open and he nearly crashed into a woman in a bright green wrap dress. A woman with light brown skin and a curvaceous, fit body, who he dimly recognized.

Shit, shit, and shit.

Her look of polite surprise rapidly dissolved into a thin-lipped look of disdain, that unfortunately accentuated her high cheekbones. She arched her eyebrow at him, her gaze filled with ice. "Huh."

She didn't need to say more. It was clear she recognized him, too. She probably didn't have any issues remembering appointments. She probably was on time for everything, always.

She'd have to be beautiful, too, damn it. No, damn his fickle memory.

A flush rose up the sides of his neck, but it wasn't his fault that he had forgotten. He pushed the bridge of his spectacles further up his nose. "Hello." Tabitha. He was terrible with names as well as appointments, but he would have known Tabitha Valby anywhere. She looked just like the pictures Anita had shown him when setting up the blind date he had foolishly forgotten. They had circled the same parties at the dance studio, always in each other's periphery, until Anita had decided to match make. She probably should have left well enough alone.

The real estate agent, whose name had also slipped Dennis's mind despite her having told him twice in the past half hour, appeared immediately with the new arrival, a tense smile on her face. "Hello! I'm Rita Foster, the real estate agent. Welcome to our open house! You aren't staying long, are you?" She flicked her gaze between him and his supposed date, as if well aware of the tension and utterly desirous of having them outside the house, no matter the financial repercussions.

The storm cloud that was his date's brow cleared infinitesimally. "Hello. I'm Tabitha Valby. I wanted to take a look, if you still have time."

Why was she asking permission? Everything about the woman seemed to radiate quiet but definite authority. Dennis had never had that confident set of his shoulders. This was a woman who commanded and was adored.

A woman who clearly despised tardiness.

Shit. Had he said *shit* already? He was not usually one for cursing.

"We absolutely must be out of here by eight, but as long as you're quick, you can take a look. Oh, and the owners have requested that no one go into the garage, so it's locked." The real estate agent, in a bright red pantsuit that dulled in comparison to the vibrant green of Tabitha's dress, gestured her inside. Dennis was clearly an afterthought, not that it was a new sensation for him. "The house was built in 1952, but the owners renovated the kitchen less than a decade ago."

With a narrow look, Tabitha Valby brushed past him to investigate the fireplace.

Dennis pushed his spectacles up the bridge of his nose again. The air she disturbed smelled like a garden center on the first warm day in May, and her stilettos echoed in the living room despite the lavish staging furniture.

Tabitha Valby.

He couldn't forget anything about her. Not now.

TABITHA HALF-LISTENED to the real estate agent's deep Philadelphia accent as she droned on about the school system and the importance of finding a good contractor for "all the little fix ups." Like Tabitha was a home renovation novice.

She would have told the agent about her family, some of the finest contractors in the Keystone state, if she hadn't been so distracted by the presence of her too-late blind date. Damn Anita for setting them up. Damn herself for listening. Tabitha was too old for this kind of shit.

After everything that had happened with Bryan, she

should have just said no to a blind date set up by her irritatingly happy dance instructor.

"I'll leave you two to look around the house while I lock up outside." Rita Foster, who needed a pantsuit that flattered her figure better, clutched her phone with white knuckles. "No dawdling. We have to be out of here by eight."

Seriously, did the house turn into a spaceship at eight? Tabitha had been there less than five minutes, and that was the third time Rita had reminded her.

Tabitha sighed, closed her eyes, and counted to ten. This could be her house. After all this time searching and getting outbid, this could be hers. Just stepping onto the land, a sense of peace had suffused her. Her parents had taught her to respect the bones of a place. Some houses were born good, some wrong. Some had the finicky personality of a Thoroughbred, requiring constant upkeep and reassurance. Others embraced a Woodstock-era vibe, laid back and hazy-eyed, willing to forgive.

This house reminded her a bit of a rescue puppy. Treat it well, and it would wait patiently for you to come home the rest of its life, wagging its tail and spreading joy. Treat it poorly, and it would chew off your face in the middle of the night.

She knew how to respect a place. This house would be hers. There was no way Damned Dennis would treat it with the love and care it deserved.

She ran a finger along the white countertop. Thank goodness it wasn't marble. Marble was for Thoroughbred houses.

"Um, Tabitha?"

She did not spare him a glance. He didn't deserve it.

Instead, she checked the cabinet underneath the kitchen sink, not out of any particular concern. The homeowners had an unexpected predilection for rat poison. Vermin wouldn't deter her from her dream home, but it could certainly help with the price point.

She heard Dennis's sigh, something breathy and sincere, and her spine stiffened. He didn't know her. He didn't know she'd never yield.

"I—I'm sorry, Tabitha."

Her heart clenched and roiled. Apologies were a dime a dozen in her experience. Bryan had "apologized" after screwing Tabitha's tennis coach, and what had it meant? Absolute zilch. "For stepping into my open house?" she asked.

He scoffed and she turned on him, arms crossed on her chest, hip jutted to the side. Her power pose, the one she practiced in the mirror a thousand times before she started her own firm.

"*Your* open house?" He pushed his spectacles up the bridge of her nose, and some long-buried, treacherous part of her found it adorable. "It's a free township. It's an *open* house."

Hah. She shoved away the softer side of her that liked that silly, sweet gesture. She had dug a grave for that part of herself years before, after The Incident.

She leaned into him and lowered her tone. "This is *my* house. I've been looking for this place for years and this has everything I want. Get out."

He ran his hands through his sandy brown hair. It reminded her of the beach and lazy summer days eating ice cream on a boardwalk. But she was not one to dwell in nostalgia. Not yet. Not until she had filled this house, with its angsty puppy vibes, with memories. Good ones.

"I will not," he said. He sounded almost prim, like he

was in a 19th century adaptation of this conversation. "I love this house. It checks every single one of my boxes."

"Every single box except the one where you neglect to show up on time for a date?"

She bit her lip. She hadn't meant to bring it up. She was fine being alone. She had only accepted the date as a favor to Anita. Since she and her partner Patrick had gotten together, they suffered from the same affliction as all happy couples, the insufferable desire to match all of their friends. And Tabitha wanted their friendship. It had been a long time since she had found a community outside her family that was so welcoming. She had needed it, after the divorce.

Dennis frowned, the crease between his light green eyes deepening like a rift in the ocean. "You're right. I should have been on time. I'm not very good with keeping appointments."

"It's not like you can set reminders on your phone or anything." She just couldn't help herself, could she? She had to keep pushing. That's what Bryan would have said, not that she cared any more.

Dennis pushed his hands into the pockets of his light gray slacks. "I already apologized. I saw this listing and the open house notification and I got too excited."

That long-buried soft part of her purred. Okay, fair point. This listing was her own personal unicorn, but she wasn't about to let him know that. "So was I, but I still showed up at the restaurant."

Dennis frowned again and pushed the spectacles back up his nose. As far as habits went, it was not the most irritating one she had ever dealt with, but she doubted he even knew he was doing it. It was utterly non-Bryan. Which was ever so slightly adorable.

Several long moments passed, with fumes practically

rising from the pair of them as they squared off across the kitchen island. She had to force them a bit, on her side. Nerdy guys had never quite done it for her before, but this one itched under her skin like poison ivy.

Tabitha narrowed her eyes at him. She was in charge of her own life. She was never going to be a victim again. She wasn't going to back down, not here, not ever.

Dennis broke the stalemate first, slumping his shoulders and casting his gaze to the vinyl-tiled kitchen floor. "Fine. I'm going to find the real estate agent. I'll get out of your hair."

He yielded? So quickly? She had been preparing for full out MMA brawl.

Tabitha almost capitulated. Almost. He was a nebbish type of cute that tugged at something deep inside of her. But no. She hadn't made it in the luxury marketing business by kowtowing. She hadn't survived The Incident and Bryan only to give up on her home ownership dream this easily.

Still. He seemed genuinely contrite. Her mother had always told her to listen to her gut when it came to people and houses.

She should confront him. She should.

Instead, she watched as he walked outside to the patio, through the full-length glass doors that opened on both sides. It would have been helpful to see the place in full daylight to get a better sense of the landscaping. She would have to talk to the real estate agent about a private showing where she could make her offer. If Dennis could find Rita. Where on Earth had she gone during her own open house?

Also, this was ridiculous, following a grown-ass man she didn't like around a house that she did. She returned to her self-tour of the premises.

She was inspecting a downstairs pantry when she heard Dennis's strained voice.

"Tabitha? Uh, Tabitha?"

One more thing she would have to manage. Clearly the man couldn't do anything properly. He could not even find the real estate agent.

Feeling somewhat justified, she sauntered into the hallway and halted directly where she stood. The swagger of smugness faded from her muscles.

He looked terrible. Not just I-fucked-up-a-blind-date terrible, but *terrible* terrible. His sandy brown hair was disheveled, and there was a high, unpleasant flush to his cheeks. She did *not* want to call the paramedics. Bryan sometimes still pulled shifts in this township. "Are you okay?" she asked.

He spoke rapidly, removing his glasses and rubbing them furiously between the folds of shirtfront. "I can't find her. I don't know where the agent went. She said she was going outside, didn't she?"

She held her hands in front of her in the same soothing gesture she used for anxious or feral animals. "Calm down, everything is going to be all right."

He glanced up and she practically recoiled at the naked fear in his green eyes. "Something doesn't feel right."

That gave Tabitha more of a pause. She was never one to discount a good old-fashioned bad vibe. Not after everything she had gone through all those years ago. She had spent years of hard-earned money on countless hours of therapy and self-defense courses in order to learn that she should never discount a bad vibe.

She placed a hand on his shoulder, surprised to feel the firmness of muscle. He wasn't a big guy, not more than a few inches taller her than her average five four, but he was wiry. Taut. Like a sexy pencil. Not that such a thing existed.

He raised his wounded gaze to hers and held it, a heartbeat in time, nothing more. A tingle swirled in the depths of her core, and she couldn't quite decide whether she was more surprised at the tingle's reappearance after so long dormant or at its provocation.

While she was decidedly *not* feeling the extent of his deltoids, the glass doors to the patio swung open. In unison, Tabitha and Dennis swerved their heads toward the sound.

Oh shit. Not again. How was this happening to Tabitha again?

Two hulking men in black tactical gear frog-marched Rita Forest, now gagged with her hands zip-tied behind her back, into the living room. Her red blazer was gone, and the white silk blouse beneath was torn up one side, the hems of her red trousers muddy and frayed. She had lost one of her shoes. Of all the things her brain could fixate on, this was the one Tabitha's chose. *Where was her goddamn shoe?* Tabitha would hate to lose her own shoes, her lucky peacock-blue stilettos. *Where was Rita's shoe?*

Tabitha's chest constricted, even as her heart galloped, the sound of her pulse in her ears so loud she could barely hear it when one of the intruders spoke. Nevertheless, it wasn't difficult to get the message. It was expected, practically rote.

Would it have killed the intruders to say something more original?

"Stay calm, or everybody dies."

3

.14159...*Shit.* Was it a five or a three? Maybe a two?

He was never going to skip a blind date again. Remembering the digits of pi typically soothed him, but it wasn't working this time.

Dennis rubbed his wrists together behind his back, wincing as the zip ties bit into his skin. Tabitha sat directly behind him, their hands so close they could touch. Under less fraught circumstances, he would not mind this at all because she smelled like clean laundry and the ocean, though not the fishy, sweaty beach like that one time he had gone with his roommates in college.

The real estate agent, Regina or Roberta or something else with an R, was sitting on the white sofa and she had not stopped crying. Dennis could understand. All that mud and blood would be a beast to clean. Baking soda and vinegar might not cut it.

The two intruders, after taking their phones and tying them up, had disappeared upstairs over an hour before. He could still hear them, their thick-soled boots thumping and clomping against the floorboards. They hadn't even wiped those boots on the mat when they came in from outside. Brutes.

He should do something. He was the man here, wasn't that what men were supposed to do? Be strong?

Cynthia would have told him what to do.

He opened his mouth to speak but a low growl from Tabitha interrupted him.

"We need to stay calm."

Of course, she would say that. She had that personality where she always said the right thing. Unlike him.

It seemed to affect the real estate agent, as her sobs became slightly less pronounced and waterlogged. Thank goodness. Crying always went straight to Dennis's lower spine, making it tense and knotted.

Tabitha spoke again, her voice more an earworm than a command. "Have you seen that video about how to escape a zip tie?"

"No." He didn't watch internet videos as he found the selection overwhelming.

"Yes," Rhonda or Rhoda said, barely above a whisper.

Great. Now he was the odd man out again.

"Rita, can you do the one where you tighten it and then lift your arms over your head?"

Rita—her name was Rita, he really needed to pay more attention with names—nodded.

"Good." Tabitha reached back until her fingers crawled against his wrists. "Dennis, I'm going to lift the shim on the locking mechanism and try to slide it free."

"I don't know what any of that means."

The force of her indubitable eye roll nearly knocked him over. "It means sit still. Once you're free, stay quiet, and get the ties off me and Rita, if she needs help."

Dennis glanced over at Rita, who was using her teeth to

tighten the zip ties so tightly, her hands swelled and whitened. With a quick, albeit shaky, movement, she lifted her arms above her head, then brought them swiftly toward her stomach, elbows outstretched like she was imitating a chicken. The zip ties snapped off her wrists.

His eyes widened, and if his hands hadn't still been tied behind his back, he would have pushed his spectacles up his nose. Wait, that worked? Did one have to be less than fifty with zero to thirty-five percent shoulder arthritis? Because Dennis was an office worker and constantly battled carpal tunnel syndrome. He needed to watch more videos instead of spending time web-sleuthing.

And of course, now his fingers were going numb because carpal tunnel was the plague of the new millennium.

Smooth, Dennis. Real smooth. He needed to focus on the current crisis at hand, like Tabitha.

Rita stood from the couch and went to the kitchen.

Tabitha's fingers were doing something around the locking mechanism of his own ties. He tried to ignore the heat in her fingers, the way the merest touch ignited something inside of him. He had never considered himself a particularly passionate or hot-blooded man, but something about the way her fingers moved definitely worked for him. Or maybe it was her innate competence.

Beads of sweat pooled around his forehead and neck.

"Stop sweating!" Tabitha hissed. "If you get the ties all slick, I won't be able to get them off."

"Let me." Rita knelt beside the pair of them, a paring knife from the kitchen block in one hand. She slipped the blade of the knife between Tabitha's ties, releasing her first before turning to Dennis.

He rubbed his now-free wrists and the three of them

huddled together. He glanced upstairs, but there was still a deal of clomping and thumping.

"Is there a phone in the house?" Tabitha asked.

Rita shook her head. Now that she was free, she had an odd air of nonchalance about her. Like she was about to have an apres-ski fondue instead of escape from home intruders. "No landline. Not here."

Dennis's heart sank. He had never become particularly attached to his phone, but now that it wasn't even an option, he felt at a loss. Also strangely ravenous for a game of Sudoku. After all, he was on quite the winning streak.

"How long do you think we have?" He matched the women's tones, checking the upstairs again even though it felt futile. Statistics said they would get caught. He never doubted statistics.

"Not long." Tabitha stood and pulled Rita and then Dennis up to join her. "We have to get out of here and to a phone. We need to call the police."

Rita was nodding, tucking strands of hair behind her ears where it had escaped her updo. "Right. Right."

"Where are your keys?" Dennis asked.

"In my purse. But the intruders took both of our purses. Where are yours?" Tabitha frowned asymmetrically, but in such a way that it made her cheekbones seem even more pronounced.

Good question. Where were his keys? What were they going to do? Dennis was never the one to turn to in situations like this, in a crisis. He never had anything useful to add, and he was terrible at finding lost things.

Except—

"Wait, my keys are behind the door."

He dashed toward the entryway cabinets where there were three small baskets, one with masks, one with shoe covers, and one for car keys. Of course his keys weren't in the basket, but he knew enough about his poor aim to keep looking. He fished behind the shelf and found his fob stuck between the basket and the wall.

"Hah! It's behind the car key basket!" He stage-whispered, showing off the key to the two women. "I never thought I'd be so grateful for my inability to throw a ball."

Rita rolled her eyes at him. "That basket isn't for car keys. That's not a thing. It was meant for business cards."

Tabitha tilted her head. "Business cards? There aren't any in that basket. Or anywhere."

A flush crimsoned Rita's neck. "I hadn't gotten around to it. This was a last-minute open house. My assistant was supposed to cancel it. I was hoping no one would show up."

A very distant part of Dennis's brain registered this was peculiar, but his primary senses focused on the rapidity of his heartbeat and likelihood of impending fatality. Statistics, after all.

Tabitha shook her head, clearly done with the exchange. Dennis had barely followed it, but at least he could follow her. She glanced upstairs, then grabbed his wrist as she exited the house, pulling him with her. She moved from the house like a ballerina, her steps light and soundless despite the stilettos she was still wearing. How did she do that?

Also, her shoes were incredible. Peacock blue and memorable, in the way most women's fashion was decidedly *not* memorable for Dennis.

He noticed she was staring at him, impatience thrumming through her posture.

"Get in the car, Dennis."

4

The man could not be more incompetent. If this were not a life or death situation, she would ditch his ass and lay pedal on her own.

In her heart, though, she knew she couldn't really do that. Neither her mother nor her conscience would let her live it down.

It took the man an eternity to unlock the damned car door, but then she and Rita piled into the passenger and back seats of his practical, rust-red sedan. Tabitha couldn't stop glancing up at the second story of the house, sure that at any moment the two intruders would run out the front door, guns blazing.

She did *not* want to die next to Dennis.

She had to remind herself that she had trained for this possibility. Escape. Focus. Survive. After The Incident...

No, she couldn't think about that now. She had to focus on Nerdy McNerderton and his bumbling escape efforts.

Dennis pulled out of the driveway slowly. At least he had the good sense to keep his headlights turned off while he reversed. Or so she had thought.

"Don't turn your headlights on until we get to the bottom of the street," Tabitha said. It wasn't too dark yet for this time in May, but the night rapidly encroached.

"How do you know they'll chase us?" Dennis's hand, mere centimeters from the headlight button, retreated to the steering wheel. In the backseat, Rita whimpered like a lost Goldendoodle.

Tabitha stared out the window, her expression hard, keeping the panicked memories at bay. Escape. Focus. Survive. "Because fuckers like that always have to have the last word."

He drove in silence for several moments, the air in the car dense with unspoken words. Outside the shadows of forest flashed by, only occasionally broken by open fields.

"Could we listen to music or something?" Rita Forest asked. That was the only way Dennis could remember her name now, in its entirety.

He gestured to Tabitha, seated beside him, who pushed the button on his dashboard and turned swiftly to the local pop station, still helmed by the same DJ he had been listening to since he was a teenager. That DJ was probably ageless.

"Did you hear about the DJ who was arrested for murdering two people thirty years ago?" he asked, his mind leap-frogging about, as it often did.

"Why on Earth would you mention that?" In the backseat, Rita Forest crossed her arms over her ruined blouse and stared out the window. "Something is wrong with you."

His jaw tightened and he took one hand off the steering wheel to readjust his spectacles. He knew that. Cynthia had said the same thing, more than twice. More than twenty times.

"Nothing is wrong with you," Tabitha said quietly. "Stress affects everyone differently. It's normal to laugh or cry or scream when you're under duress. Take time to process it however you need."

Rita Forest guffawed in the backseat.

Dennis watched in the rearview mirror as Tabitha turned, cutting Rita Forest with her gaze. A strange lightness pulled at the center of his chest.

Tabitha turned and stared out the windshield, the muscles of her face tight. "And yes, I did hear about that DJ. It's amazing, the work the police are doing to solve cold cases."

There must have been an entire herd of wild horses galloping through his chest. "Exactly! I've been volunteering, you know, as a genealogist." He clapped his mouth shut, certain that he had said the wrong thing. Cynthia had never liked the long hours he had spent after coming home from the accounting firm, searching through family records and newspaper articles, trying to piece people's history back together. But it suited him, suited his mathematical mind, suited his social anxiety.

"Really?" Tabitha replied. He liked having her attention on him. It did something to his skin, made it feel like a glowing light instead of just the dry, itchy thing he forgot to moisturize. She really did have lovely eyes. "Do you work with any police officers? Anyone we might be able to contact?"

Dennis's face fell. He had, of course, completely forgotten the situation at hand, which was far more dire than Dennis-needs-a-date. "No. Sorry. I'm more of an armchair volunteer."

A chill descended in the car as he lost her attention. Trees and street signs whipping by were more interesting than he was. He should not be surprised.

"Why are we heading south?" Tabitha finally asked.

"How do you know where we're going?" Rita Forest's voice piped in from the backseat. He had almost thought she had fallen asleep.

Tabitha gestured to the rearview mirror, which boasted a digital *S* in the top right corner. "We could have headed to the restaurant. It's only a ten-minute drive east of here."

A flush of regret pulsed through him. Five minutes with Tabitha, and he was convinced he would always regret forgetting their date. "I don't know where it is, and I don't have GPS or a phone." He pushed his spectacles up his nose. He really ought to get them fixed. "I don't want to get lost. I figure if we drive south we will either hit Delaware or Maryland. A lot sooner than if we headed into Philadelphia."

"Why not west? Lancaster isn't far."

He sniffed. "I've gotten stuck behind too many buggies or trucks. I thought this would be faster."

"It would be," Tabitha said, her voice a murmur. "If you drove more than eight miles over the speed limit."

"No one is following us! There's no one else even on the road." He took one hand off the wheel only to gesture at the austerity of the environs. "Safety comes first." A light flared on his dash, just beneath his odometer. "Shoot. And gas. We need to get gas."

Tabitha arched her pretty eyebrows at him. "Shoot? Who says 'shoot?'" She used air quotes, actual air quotes.

He would not deign to remove his hands from ten and two. "'Shoot' is a perfectly acceptable word."

"In whose parlance? 'Shoot' is for school marms and nonagenarians in 1902."

"That's hardly true. I know plenty of people who say 'shoot.'" He couldn't think of any at the moment, but he was certain they existed.

"Are they nonagenarians from 1902?"

"There weren't that many nonagenarians in 1902 because human life expectancy wasn't more than fifty years old!"

"Why do you even know the average life expectancy in 1902?" She crossed her arms over her chest. He felt the heat of her gaze burning into him.

He never got this upset about anything. Ever. He never felt this rise in his pulse, this fire through his veins. But he liked it. He felt the same way he had when he had danced in his first ballroom competition. *Seen.* "Because I do. Because the 19th century was a cesspit of pollution and disease and classism and they didn't have the benefit of penicillin or vaccines."

He chanced a glance at her. Her posture was tense, but pensive, her rosebud lips pursed. Rosebud lips? He never thought in such poetic terms.

"Nothing to say to that, hmm?" He was baiting her, actually baiting her. He never did this. Something had clearly possessed him.

"I mean, technically, the history of vaccination began well before the 18th century of Edward Jenner's supposed 'discovery—'" she inserted a gesture between air quotes and jazz hands—" of cowpox variolation to prevent smallpox. There are earlier accounts of people in Africa and Asia using inoculation techniques to prevent against disease. It's yet one more example of western Europe trying to co-opt all major discoveries." She kept her gaze straightforward, then turned to look at him, her eyes warm and sparkling. He melted under her attention, as if she were the sun and he a leftover piece of Halloween chocolate. "I concede you are correct about the timeline for the discovery of penicillin."

His heart leapt and stopped, leapt and stopped again. What was it like to breathe? It felt so long since he had done anything remotely resembling it.

He heard the rumble of the reminder strips on the side of the road and veered back into his lane.

"I have to pee," Rita Forest said.

His focus crashed back to their present situation. This was not the time for flirtation with a sexy, smart woman. Unfortunately.

He glanced in the rearview mirror and saw Rita Forest squirming on her seat.

"Okay. We hopefully should be crossing a major road soon. We'll stop at a gas station, refuel, and see if we can use their phone." His eyes widened in shock. He never had such a cool, comprehensive plan that had nothing to do with numbers. He inhaled deeply and turned to the woman in the passenger seat. "What do you think, Tabitha?"

He felt the ice in her gaze. Uh oh. What had he done wrong this time? He had not meant to offend her. Indubitably she had a better plan. Maybe he was mansplaining, though he did not fully understand what that entailed. He did understand that women *hated* mansplaining.

If only he had his phone so he could look it up and make sure he didn't do that with Tabitha.

"How do you have money to pay for gas?" she asked, eyebrow arched.

He flushed. "Oh. I keep an emergency prepaid debit card in my glovebox." In case he ever got carjacked, he would have something to offer. But that didn't seem the sort of thing he ought to say out loud.

"Hmm" was all the response he received. At least he hadn't mansplained. The instant this whole thing was over and he had internet access, he would search for what that term meant.

5

Tabitha needed to get out of this slow-ass car with this oddly charming drip of a guy and back to her real life. Immediately. Out of nearly three decades of dating, this was by far the worst blind date she had ever had, and that was counting the guy who had shown up in a full knight's costume complete with sword and the guy who had vomited into the vintage luxury clutch she had scrimped and saved for, and then still had the gall to ask her for sex.

Yes. This trumped them all.

Even if the way Dennis looked at her made her feel like she was some sort of ancient Greek goddess of power and intelligence.

She glanced out the window to distract herself from Dennis's laser focus, and she caught a flash of blue light reflected against the pane.

She spun in her seat, so fast she could have torn her old whiplash injury anew. "Is that a phone?"

"No!" Rita looked aghast, but her voice trembled like the whiny trill of a cicada. "Of course not. They took our phones. Remember?" She accented the second syllable like she was a damned fourteen-year-old.

As her grandmother would say, Tabitha had not been born yesterday. There was something suspicious about the weird timing of the open house and the agent's eagerness to be rid of them. What if Rita was in on the home invasion? Women were supposed to help other women, but Tabitha knew well how low that bar really was. "Rita—"

"There's a gas station up ahead."

She turned as Dennis spoke and saw the reassuring neon red blazing through the night sky. The suspicion growing at the base of her neck dulled. A gas station. Who knew salvation was open twenty-four hours, offered radioactive burritos, and had a bathroom that had probably seen some S.H.I.T? No "Shoots" for Tabitha. No sir.

"Wait." She put a hand on his arm as he was about to put on his indicator lights. He glanced at her, then pulled the car onto the side of the road and idled. Wow. A man who listened right away. Bryan would have completely mansplained her.

An old Rod Stewart song was playing on the radio, drowning out the cicadas that descended early this year.

"What's wrong?" Dennis whispered.

Rita leaned forward between the two front seats. "Why are we whispering?"

Tabitha rolled her eyes. "I just want to make sure no one else is coming."

Dennis nodded and Rita flopped back into her seat, crossing her arms over her chest again. The woman was Tabitha's age but acted like her eight-year-old niece.

Tabitha couldn't deal with her now. Escape. Focus. Call police. That was what she needed to accomplish.

She glanced over at the gas station. There weren't any

other cars at any of the pumps. A beat-up pickup truck was parked near the back of the lot, so it likely belonged to the cashier. Hopefully there was a phone inside. She hadn't seen a working pay phone in over a decade.

"I don't see anyone on the roads," she said at last, realizing that both Dennis and Rita seemed to be waiting on her. For the life of her, she couldn't figure out why. She had no interest in being the leader of this motley group. None. She one hundred percent did *not* need another relationship in her lifetime built on surviving an attack. Been there, done that, had the divorce papers to prove it.

Damn it, they were still waiting for her. "I guess it's okay to go inside. Let's just be quick."

"Good. I have to pee so badly." The realtor seemed barely bothered by being tied up and on the run.

Tabitha sighed inwardly at the TMI but managed to keep her composure. Escape. Focus. Survive. "You use the restroom while Dennis pumps gas, and I'll get a phone to call the police."

Dennis's shoulders visibly relaxed. She hadn't realized he was so tense, but maybe he was the kind of guy who liked taking orders.

She didn't particularly mind giving them.

Nope, she had to remind herself how toxic things had gotten between her and Bryan. She was Tabitha Valby. She did not repeat the mistakes of her past.

Dennis pulled back onto the empty street and turned into the gas station parking lot.

"Everything will be all right soon," he whispered, likely to himself. Wishes and prayers. Preparation and adaptability, that was better. Tabitha had learned long ago never to take any moment for granted. Things could go to shit in a heartbeat.

No sooner had he parked in front of one of the gas pumps than Rita was out of the car and dashing into the convenience store. "I guess she really did have to pee." Dennis took the gas card from the glovebox, stepped from the car, and opened the door to the gas tank.

Tabitha's heart pounded in her chest, so strong she wondered if she might be getting atrial fibrillation like in those commercials during the late-night TV she liked. No, she could do this. Escape. Focus. Call police. Survive.

She stepped out of the car and shivered in her green dress. The night had taken a cool turn. Rain was coming, she was almost certain of it. She should have just stayed home in her sweatpants, but she couldn't second guess all of her choices. Therapy had taught her that.

No time to dither. There was an old metal pay phone casing, *sans* phone, standing near the propane containers and the fill-your-own water container station. The metal sides of were dented and nearly every inch was covered in a mixture of colorful graffiti and swear words in permanent marker. She sighed. She hadn't really counted on a pay phone, anyway, and it wasn't like she had change. Everyone she knew paid for everything on their phones or with credit cards.

She glanced over her shoulder at Dennis, who frowned at the gas card in his hand.

"Everything all right?"

"I have to go inside to pay." He met her gaze, his bright green eyes vibrant in the neon lights. "I guess they don't let you use gas cards at the pump."

She shrugged, ignoring the sense of relief at having company.

She straightened her shoulders and pushed open the plexiglass door of the convenience store. Blinking against the neon flare, she made her way to the drinks fridge. Might as well peruse the assortment of sparkling waters.

She watched Dennis, reflected in the doors of the drinks fridge. He went directly to the clerk, an older woman with a frizzy gray mullet and a dull maroon work vest.

"Hello." Dennis used the same voice she used when one of her subordinates had fucked something to hell and back and now she had to fix everything. She begrudgingly had to admit it was a little sexy. "I have an emergency. I need to use your phone, immediately."

The woman cracked her gum and raised one bushy gray eyebrow at him. There was a huge nacho cheese stain smeared across the shoulder of her plain black T-shirt. "We don't have a pay phone here." Tabitha moved across to the iced tea selection.

"I'm aware of that. It's an emergency. My—my friends and I were in a home invasion. We need to call the police."

Tabitha watched as Dennis pushed his spectacles so far up his nose the wire frame nearly impaled him.

The clerk rolled her eyes. "Seriously? It's not even nine thirty. Guess the drunks are out early tonight."

"I have not been drinking. We need to call the police. The intruders took our cell phones."

Tabitha ignored the stale hair band music pumping through the store. She could see Dennis grip the counter tightly, his knuckles turning pale white.

The clerk sat down on her stool. "Look, buddy, I've heard everything. I've worked graveyard for eight years now. We don't have phones, especially if you're not a customer."

"Just give me your goddamn phone!" Dennis screamed, a tone clearly unfamiliar to him as his entire body immediately flushed the red of a well-cooked lobster.

Tabitha arched an eyebrow. She kind of liked it when he lost his cool.

The clerk was unphased. She rolled her eyes, cracked her gum, and lifted her hands in a peaceful gesture. "I'll call them. I'll tell them you're disturbing the peace."

Even Tabitha rolled her eyes. For fuck's sake. Poor Dennis.

"Fine, please. Go ahead, tell them I'm the problem here." Dennis sighed, so loudly it drowned out the buzz from the drinks fridge. "Just call them."

The clerk gestured toward his hip, which was nearly half a foot from the candy bar display. "Don't touch the counter, please." Moving so slowly she might have been part sloth, the clerk removed an old model cell phone from the pocket of her ancient mom jeans.

Tabitha scoffed and joined Dennis, patting his shoulder. "It's all right, honey."

A smile flitted across his face. It was a rather nice face.

At least this grump was calling the police. At least this night would be over soon. Tabitha could give her statement, go home, have a huge glass of malbec and a hot bath, and forget any of this had ever happened.

She glanced toward the bathroom door, which was still closed. Rita was taking an unusually long time. Maybe she was getting herself cleaned up after her encounter with the intruders. She would give her another few minutes. *Some* people could be patient with one another. Tabitha cut a look at the clerk but the woman ignored her. She was still typing on her phone. "It doesn't take that long to type 911," Tabitha said.

"If you're going to pester me, I won't do it," the clerk shot back. "Take your boyfriend and leave me alone."

Fine. Whatever. She let the boyfriend remark slide, but

saw Dennis flush anew. Something deep in her stomach clenched and flopped. It was pretty adorable, how nebbish he was.

"Um, miss," he said, stuttering. "I need gas on pump—"

"I'll be with you in a minute," the cashier snapped back.

Tabitha glanced out the window, taking in the fallen night, the neon lights, Dennis's sedan. This would be over soon.

Then Tabitha's eyes widened.

Twin flares approached rapidly, the lights enlarging as they neared the station.

Shit.

Tabitha seized Dennis's hand, looping her fingers between his.

"What's wrong?" he asked. She knew she squeezed too tightly but did not care.

Tabitha grabbed his arm and pulled him deeper into the store. There had to be an exit. Somewhere they could watch and see who was coming. There was a possibility it wasn't the home intruders. A remote possibility. Escape. Focus. Survive.

She pushed Dennis toward a metal door with an EXIT sign swinging above it.

"Hey, that's for employees only!" the clerk shouted.

Of all the nights to have the world's worst clerk. Tabitha sighed and released the metal doorknob.

"What's wrong?" Dennis repeated, his hand clutching hers.

She went to the bathroom door and rapped on it. "Rita!" she hissed. "Rita! We have to go!"

"Just a moment!" the real estate agent called, her voice singsongy and completely unsuited to the current situation.

The nerves at the base of Tabitha's spine tingled. Something wasn't right. Not with Rita Forest. Not with this situation. "We don't have a moment! Get out here!"

Over the shelves of chips and snacks, Tabitha saw the car pull into the gas station lot and park directly outside the doors. It was a black SUV, a large one. The kind used by nefarious people. Her heartbeat sped anew. She crouched behind a display of corn chips and Dennis knelt beside her.

"The police will be here in ten minutes," the clerk called to them.

Tabitha did her best to quiet her racing thoughts. Her mother had always said to listen to her instincts, and every single nerve in her body was telling her they didn't have ten minutes. They shouldn't trust the clerk. They shouldn't trust Rita.

But Dennis? She examined him closely, listening to her inner voice. It told her maybe he was dependable. Even if he was a bit feckless, he radiated loyalty, honor.

Escape. Focus. Survive.

"Dennis—" She turned to tell him they shouldn't wait. Not for the cops. Not for Rita. But when she caught his gaze, she saw comprehension. Comprehension, understanding, and complete and total agreement. Trustworthy.

As one, they started moving toward the rear exit of the convenience store, keeping their bodies low.

"Didn't you hear me?" The clerk waved at them from behind the desk. "What are you doing?" Tabitha didn't look but could hear the simultaneous opening of the bathroom door and the tinkling of the bell over the glass entry. They didn't have time. Her heartbeat skyrocketed.

Dennis squeezed her hand, and before she could fully process the situation, she and Dennis made a run for the exit.

Escape. Focus. Call police. Survive.

"Stop them!" a deep, male voice said behind them.

Rita, whom Tabitha could see in the periphery of her gaze, reached for Tabitha's arm, but Tabitha side-stepped and elbowed the real estate agent, barely registering the thwump of bone on flesh.

"You bitch!" Rita shouted, her voice pitchy. "I am going to kill you!"

Good thing Tabitha listened to her instincts. Not that she had time to dwell on that now.

She and Dennis flung themselves out of the rear employee exit door, setting off the peal of an emergency alarm. They bolted across the empty parking lot. Tabitha was sure her steps were winged, as she had never run so fast in her entire life, certainly not in a designer wrap dress that she had selected for style over function.

Without speaking, Dennis seemed to understand Tabitha's plan. He matched her, pace for pace, as she dashed into the forest behind the station. Barely pausing to register the action, she kicked off the heels that slowed her down. She hoped like hell she wouldn't regret it.

Escape. Focus. Survive.

Behind her, she heard the heavy pounding of boots on pavement, men swearing, Rita still screaming and calling their names.

Escape. Focus. Survive.

They ran blindly, branches whipping at their faces, arms held up in a vain effort to block the twigs from stabbing them as they went. Deeper and deeper into the forest they ran.

Tabitha's chest was on fire. Her lungs ached as if they were a dying bellows, and her legs, whose strength she had always admired, felt like they were made of strawberry jam.

"I have to stop," Dennis wheezed beside her.

Grateful but still cautious, Tabitha slowed her gait. She glanced around them to clock her surroundings.

She didn't know how long it had been, how far they had run, where they even were. The main road was a distant memory, not a single streetlight in sight. On the other hand, their pursuers were nowhere to be found, either.

Dennis hunched over, hands on his knees, coughing and wheezing. His face was bright red, but at least he still had his spectacles.

"Are you okay?" She placed a hand on his back, reveling momentarily in his warmth. He nodded in lieu of answering.

She kept her eyes peeled for sight of the intruders, but it seemed they had lost them in their mad dash. Heaving, she leaned against the trunk of a sugar maple and tried to catch her breath.

"So." Dennis looked up, breathing in between each word. The redness of his face had softened, particularly in the dim starlight. Even wherever they were out in the forest, there was light pollution, but it lent a pleasant, other-worldly air to everything. "Where do you think we are?"

6

Dennis watched as Tabitha shrugged, but not in a helpless way. More of a "No, I don't know where we are at this moment but give me ten minutes and I will build a compass from a hair pin and a leaf" kind of shrug. He wondered if he should tell her that with the exertion, the wrap of her dress had loosened and now the green fabric gaped, exposing a hint of her soft skin.

He gazed up at the stars, anything to avoid staring so openly at her. She really was lovely, certainly one of the most beautiful women he had ever seen. Cynthia had been pretty, petite with a little brunette pixie cut that she would spike at will. He had never known a woman like Tabitha, though, every inch of her oozing confidence and elegance.

Dennis, of course, had sweat stains the size of Jupiter and Uranus under his arms and down his back. If he had known he was going to run for his life, he would have chosen one of his cotton polo shirts instead of a sweater vest/Oxford shirt combo.

The absurdity of dressing for danger made him chortle-snort. He clapped a hand over his mouth. "Shoot. I am so sorry."

This was mortifying. Here he was, practically ready to worship at her feet, and then he ruined everything with a chortle-snort.

"It's okay." He heard the smile in her voice before he saw it. It lightened her features, lifted her cheekbones, and made her dark brown eyes sparkle. "Was that a chortle-snort?"

"Um, yes." He didn't think anyone else had ever called it that before. "I—I do it sometimes, when I get nervous or surprised."

She nodded. She seemed to have finally caught her breath, and her posture was now more relaxed. She wrapped her arms around herself. "I had a friend in college who used to do that. It was adorable. You always knew exactly where you stood with her, with a laugh that distinctive. It's honest."

He had never thought of it that way. He had never really considered at all that it would be some sort of boon instead of curse. Or its relationship to his inability to lie. It was true, though, now that he thought about it. If he wasn't truly delighted, he forced a tiny, polite, society-appropriate chuckle.

The cloud that had been covering the three-quarters moon shifted, limning her in the light, the shadows highlighting her features. He could have looked at her forever.

"Are you cold?" he asked.

"No." But even from this distance, he caught the shiver.

"Here." He fumbled a bit, as he wasn't very good at removing his clothes in front of people, but he managed to remove his shirt while keeping the sweater vest where it belonged. Small victory. "It's a little sweaty, but at least it's warm."

She stared at him, eyes wide, mouth partially open. Dennis felt the flush along his entire spine. He shouldn't have thought this was a good idea. What beautiful woman wanted a used sweaty shirt? Was this as bad as mansplaining? Why did he never understand the fine points of appealing to the opposite sex?

"I'm sorry." He inspected the forest floor so maybe she wouldn't see his mortification. As if that were possible. For the first time, he noticed that she had ditched her heels and had been running barefoot through the forest. He should offer her his shoes, too, though those undoubtedly had an off-putting odor, and there had to be an unspoken rule about never sharing shoes. His shirt hung limply from one hand and he shivered in the cool night breeze. "It was stupid of me. I shouldn't have thought you would want it."

"No, thank you." She approached him and covered his hand, the one holding the Oxford, with her own. Warmth ricocheted up his arm and he couldn't tear his gaze from where they connected. "I appreciate it."

With that, she stepped away from him, breaking the hold and plunging Dennis into an icy bath of regret. He watched as she shrugged into the button-down shirt, which hung in a peculiarly appealing way around her curves.

Something stirred deep inside of him, but what it was, he couldn't tell. It wasn't pure desire. He had felt that before. This was something new, something stronger, something longer-lasting. He liked it.

"So," she said, her voice melodious in a way that sliced slowly through him. "Which way should we go?"

Right. He kept forgetting where they were and what they were doing. He needed to focus on the task at hand, not on how her presence warmed him to his very core.

He turned slowly in a circle, calculating. This was math,

probability. He just had to figure out which direction had the highest likelihood of success.

He blinked several times. How in the world did someone do that when they were completely lost? There was something about the North Star, but he couldn't guarantee he hadn't seen that in a movie. Besides, clouds filled the night sky, obscuring the landmarks.

"Maybe we should head back toward the gas station." He gestured vaguely in what he hoped was the proper direction. "If the clerk already called the police, they've surely arrived by now. We'd be done, saved."

He put his hands on his hips, smiling. Yes, this was definitely a good plan. He was proud he had thought of it. Maybe she would—

Then he noticed her slowly shaking her head. The flush of shame crept up his neck again. *Here it comes.* He knew what to expect, the derision, the casual rejection of his well-thought out suggestion.

"I don't know." Tabitha crossed her arms over her chest as she stared in the direction he was indicating. "You talked to that clerk. Have you ever met a less helpful person? If she even did make the phone call, I doubt she told the police anything useful."

What sort of person refused to help someone else? No one Dennis would associate with, that was certain. Though the gas station cashier had been a particular brand of awful. "What about Rita Forest?" He stuck his hands in his pockets, absurdly proud he had actually recalled her name. "We left her back there. She could be waiting for us."

Tabitha arched an eyebrow at him. "Your naivete is adorable, but not helpful in this situation."

Every part of his skin, from his scalp to his toes, flushed beet red. Had she just called him adorable?

She did not seem to register his distress. "Didn't you see her? I thought she had a phone in the car, and I'll bet anything I was right. She tried to grab me as I ran past the bathroom. I'll wager she was in on it all from the start. She probably called the intruders when she went to the bathroom. It took her a ridiculous amount of time to pee."

Dennis never measured how long it took any lady in the restroom. He understood that it was one of those feminine mysteries he would never comprehend, and so he had no bar for this assessment, unlike Tabitha. Besides, he would have agreed with just about anything Tabitha said at that point. If she had said purple unicorns rained from the sky on odd Tuesdays, he would have bought a titanium umbrella in preparation.

"Okay, no gas station." He crossed it off mentally in his head, even if he was a little sorry to see it go and take their chances on foot. *The devil you know and all that.* "Then what do you think?"

For several moments, they both turned in circles, each slow, calculating. Dennis matched Tabitha's pace, speed, and movements, searching for...something. Anything. Anything to make sense of the dark. No matter where he looked, everything looked the same, everything smelled and sounded the same. His heart fluttered wildly in his chest. Nowhere he turned held anything more than shadows and uncertainty.

Finally, she stopped her rotation, palms held in front of her as though they carried a divining rod. "I can't tell an anthill from Adam right now, but this seems as good a try as any."

7

Dennis helped her over an enormous tree branch. She let herself linger for the briefest of moments, his hands steady on the sides of her chest. A flash of heat ricocheted through her.

No. This was a bad idea. Relationships forged in traumatic circumstances were doomed to failure. And had she forgotten how he had ditched her at the restaurant? Though the more time she spent with him, she suspected he genuinely had forgotten the appointment. He gave every indication that he wouldn't forget her so easily now.

Again. Bad idea. Escape. Focus. Survive. That was the plan.

She turned back to the path they were making and wiped her hands on her clothes. Not that she would have done that in her daily life. Hands told multitudes about a person, and she always kept hers clean. "What are the odds we find the one wood in southeastern Pennsylvania with not one human being for miles?"

Dennis flushed. Grinning, Tabitha pointed at him. "You know, don't you?"

He shoved his hands in his pockets and kicked a large fallen branch out of their path. "I—okay, yes. Yes, I do."

She nudged him playfully, unable to repress her amusement. Without roads around, there was a diminished risk of the intruders finding them, and her heart felt a bit lighter. "Be proud of that! My mother always said never to hide my own intelligence. You could take a cue from her."

He glanced at her, something flaring in his eyes, then turned his gaze back to the ground. With one arm, he lifted a particularly vicious-looking thorny branch and she passed underneath, unscathed.

They walked in silence for a few moments. Tabitha clutched the shirt more tightly around her. Now that they were no longer being actively pursued, her heart rate had returned to a more normal decibel, and the lack of adrenaline left her chilled and exhausted. She had to muscle through it, that was all.

She hadn't expected to enjoy the company, though. Something about Dennis crept under her skin. It should have disconcerted her.

Instead, it made her feel more like herself.

"You know, I think this is the first time in my adult life where I don't know where I'm going." She shook her head, enjoying the freedom of the breeze through her long, dark locks. The night smelled clean and fresh, like a recently-staged house. All that was missing was the aroma of baking cookies.

Her stomach grumbled.

"I'm sorry. I should have grabbed something to eat from the convenience store." Dennis helped her over another fallen log, even lifting the hem of her green dress when it snagged a thick piece of shaggy bark.

She laughed, the sound startling in the quiet evening. A

bird flapped its wings loudly and the pair of them turned toward the fluttering.

"You mean you should have had the wherewithal to grab a bag of chips when we were running for our lives? Give yourself a break, Dennis. I'm a grown woman. I can take care of myself. It's just that I don't think I've eaten since lunch."

"I know you can take care of yourself." He hesitated. "You would have eaten if I had showed up at the restaurant. I am so sorry I missed our date. I can be really scatter-brained about things like that. Cynthia never liked that either."

He placed his hand on her elbow, so gently it felt like a breath of smoke, then as quickly he returned it to his pocket. He raced forward a few paces and tossed a pile of brush out of the path.

This was getting interesting. It didn't particularly help that Dennis looked rather adorable in the moonlight, the white rays darkening his brow and shifting through his eyes, making them glow like green embers in a fire.

"Who's Cynthia?"

He flushed and pushed his spectacles up his nose. "She was my fiancée."

He said it matter-of-factly, like he was reporting a meteo-rological statistic. Intriguing. "I'm sorry."

He shrugged, his slender, strong shoulders visible under the sweater vest. The man worked *out*.

"It's all right. I was really upset about it for a while. Which I guess makes sense. But now I think it was probably for the best."

Warmth spread through her that had exactly nothing to do with the current temperature. "Did you love her? Did she break your heart?"

"I don't know. She was my only girlfriend, really. We had been together for three years, and she kept saying neither of us was getting any younger." He frowned and she shuddered at the rush of fire along her spine. He had a definite Clark Kent thing going for him. "I think, now that I look back on it, we wanted different things."

She understood that. Her prior relationships had been studies in the opposites-attract trope. Which had worked out *so* well for her. "Like what?"

He paused along the path, then removed his spectacles and cleaned them with the hem of his sweater vest. He exhaled, a sigh so deep it sounded like he was releasing his soul. "I don't know. I've always wanted...someone. But I've never been good with a lot of people. I probably shouldn't say this, but I've always been really hesitant about having kids. And Cynthia wanted all of that. She wanted a big house, to entertain, and exactly three children. I just wanted a person. My person. Someone to come home to and go to dinner with. Someone who understood me. Someone who liked me for me."

It was a lovely idea. That was all she had wanted once, too. Before The Incident and Bryan and—

Tabitha shifted from foot to foot. Ditching her shoes had seemed a good idea at the time, but after hiking barefoot through the forest, her feet made their irritation known.

Dennis gestured to a large nearby rock and she perched atop it, grateful for the rest. He knelt in front of her. "Is it all right if I wrap your feet? They look like they hurt. I'd give you my shoes, but I don't think they'd fit you."

Her heart leapt and rolled in some sort of gymnastic routine. Who was this gentleman and from which school of enlightenment had he graduated? "Um, sure. Thank you."

He took one foot in his hands, and with the same gentleness and care someone would show to a frightened animal, he glided his fingertips along the raw surface of her sole. She had anticipated the protest of raw nerve endings, but instead his touch was whisper-light and soothing.

She closed her eyes and moaned. He removed a handkerchief from his pocket, tore it in half, and wrapped each of her feet with the cool fabric. Dear Lord, it was absolute sheer heaven. "Cynthia must have been a fool. This is amazing."

She wasn't too delirious that she missed his flush of pleasure. "I'm glad you like it. Cynthia never let me touch her like this."

"Her loss."

He adjusted the wrappings to cover the worst injuries. When he hit a particularly sensitive spot, she hissed, drawing her bottom lip through her teeth.

"Too hard?"

"No, no, keep going. Thank you so much for this."

He continued, his head turned toward his ministrations. "So, um, what about you? Have you ever been married?"

Good things never did last. She straightened up and moved her feet from his incredible hands. All these years later and she didn't know what to tell people. Damn Bryan. "Thank you for the wrappings. My feet feel much better now."

"Oh, okay." He scrambled to a stand and shoved his hands in his pockets. "I hope I didn't hurt you."

"Not at all." She smiled broadly, but knew it was brittle. She slipped off the rock, but then turned, the tiny hairs on the back of her neck standing to attention.

"Unless I'm completely hallucinating, I think I hear music." She pointed, southwest to the path they were currently taking. It was a shift in the sounds of the forest night, a melody. It called to her.

He looped her arm in his and helped her over an enormous deadfall blocking the path. "I am at your disposal, Tabitha. Wherever you go, I'll follow."

She closed her eyes and hummed. Just the sound of her name on his lips was almost as good as the free foot massage he had given her. She could just imagine how those hands would feel, ministering to her other aches and pains.

She needed to pull it together. They were in danger. She couldn't let him pull her focus. They were out alone, in the cold dark forest, without phones or wallets or keys, being chased by two intruders with nefarious intentions. What was she doing, daydreaming about Senor Nerdalicious beside her? She needed to find a phone, some food, and some warm shelter, not a boyfriend. Survival. That was the goal.

Definitely not a boyfriend.

8

The music strengthened as they neared. It wasn't a tune Dennis was familiar with, but it filled him with lightness, making him feel buoyant and young. Bizarrely, as he really wasn't a big drinker, he had the oddest urge for pretzels and beer.

Tabitha's steps quickened beside him. She must feel it too, the hope of their imminent salvation. Soon she would be rid of him and could go back to her life, her real life. One without home invasions and negligent blind dates.

Dennis pushed his spectacles up his nose. He shouldn't have told her about Cynthia. Women didn't like hearing about other women, did they? Or maybe he shouldn't have asked if she had been married before.

He sighed. If only he had more practice talking to beautiful women.

She grabbed his arm, her excitement palpable, and transferred it to him through their connection. He liked the way she felt, like she wanted to be there.

"I see it! There's a building! Look!"

He followed the path she indicated. He could see it, too.

A light clapboard house with friendly yellow light gleaming from its light-shuttered windows. The joyful, playful, and energetic music streamed from the house.

Maybe it was a mirage.

"Come on!" Tabitha grabbed his arm and started running.

He faltered, then shook his head. They had come this far together. He didn't know how long it had been or what else lay ahead of them, but if he could just spend five more minutes with her...that's all he wanted. Five more minutes.

He dashed after her.

TABITHA'S SMILE widened the closer she got to the VFW, and her pace grew faster. Dennis huffed and puffed not far behind her.

A woman with strawberry blond hair in two coiled braids stood beside a tiny red hatchback, her petticoats and frilled dress limned by the car lights. She carried a giant bowl with what looked like potato salad, and she kicked the car door shut with one foot.

Hoping like hell she didn't scare off her chance of salvation, Tabitha raised her hand toward the woman while not slowing her pace. "Hello!"

The woman turned sharply, fumbling with the side dish. She balanced it on one forearm and placed one hand on her brow, like she was trying to make sense of the shapes in the darkness. "Hello?"

Relief flooded through her as Tabitha careened out of the tree line. "Hi, I am so sorry to bother you." Her breath heaved and her feet ached beyond reason but she couldn't stop. The woman had a pretty spray of freckles across her cheeks and light-colored eyes wherein the lights from the VFW played and cavorted.

"Can I help you?"

"I'm Tabitha Valby." She pointed as Dennis skidded to a heaving stop beside her. "This is Dennis. Please, can we use your phone? It's an emergency. We were in a home invasion, and they took everything." Tears pricked at the backs of her eyes and she swallowed a lump in her throat. *Please, let this work.* Beside her, Dennis clenched and unclenched his fists repeatedly.

The woman covered her mouth with the hand not balancing potato salad. "Are you serious? A home invasion?"

"Yes." Dennis gestured to the bowl. "That looks heavy. Can I help you with that?" An easy smiled crossed the woman's face, though her brow was knit with concern. She passed Dennis the bowl.

"Please." Tabitha pressed her palms together, praying to the woman and anyone else who was listening. "We've been out here, walking. We need to call the police."

"Oh my goodness, of course! I'm sorry I hesitated. It's awful." The strawberry blonde with excellent fashion sense smiled and gestured at the open door. Every muscle in Tabitha's body unclenched. "Come on inside. I left my phone in there, and you two look like you could use a rest." The woman gestured toward the door.

What was this magical place where people were actually helpful? Tabitha smoothed her skirt and readjusted the fall of her dress against her chest. She had never looked so unkempt in her entire life, but at least she knew now this would be temporary.

"I'm Phoebe," the woman said, following them inside and shutting the door behind them. "You can put the potato salad on the buffet table." She pointed Dennis to two long picnic tables shoved together under red-and-white checked tablecloths. They practically overflowed with food, chafing dishes with bratwurst and sauerkraut, slow cookers bubbling with stews, and an entire table dedicated to different German-looking cakes. Tabitha had seen more than one baking competition show, and these were next-level gorgeous. She hoped she wasn't salivating openly. "Just move things around a bit and make some space." Phoebe turned to Tabitha. "You can rest here. We're still setting up for tonight."

Tabitha sank into the folding chair Phoebe indicated, her feet practically crying out in gratitude. "Thank you so much. What is all of this?"

"Oh, it's our monthly Polka Party." Phoebe twirled, her pink polka-dotted dress flaring around her legs.

A polka party? Tabitha glanced around the room. She would roll with it. "Everyone looks wonderful. The dresses are fantastic."

"Thank you!" Phoebe perched on a chair nearby and pulled a voluminous pink tote bag emblazoned with thick black letters, POLKA PROBLEM. "A lot of us make them ourselves. Leah over there has an online store. She ships all over the world. It's amazing." She rifled through the contents of the tote bag for several minutes. "I know it's in here somewhere. Aha!" She brandished a cell phone in a bright pink and purple polka-dotted case. Tabitha respected a woman with a theme. "Here you go."

Tabitha held the phone as if it were made of diamonds. Her hands trembled. She exhaled deeply, then swiped Phoebe's phone screen to activate the emergency call. It rang in her ear, the toll shuddering through her entire body.

Good. This was good. They had escaped. They had found help. Now she could call the police and go home.

Dennis returned from the buffet table, his hands in his pockets. He watched her intently. She tried to telegraph a comforting smile, but her heart was throbbing.

A click and a deep voice rumbled over the line. "911."

Was that how 911 answered calls? "Hello!" Shit, she sounded way too eager. Who was she kidding? Of course she was eager to be done with tonight. "Hi. Yes, thank you. My name is Tabitha Valby. My friend Dennis and I were in a home invasion at an open house. Address was 6267 Lightman Terrace in Lewis, Pennsylvania. The men have been chasing us." A sob clenched in her throat and she shook her head. She hadn't lost her cool the last time she had endured trauma, and she wouldn't now. "Please. Please help us. I don't know where we are."

"Ma'am, please take a deep breath."

Irritation rankled through her. She was calm enough, thank you damn much, particularly in light of the events of her evening. Beside her, Dennis covered her hand with his, and a very small amount of the tension dissipated from her shoulders.

"Ma'am, can you tell me anything about where you are?"

That was odd. Shouldn't 911 have GPS? She checked the phone screen briefly to make sure she had, indeed, called emergency services.

It seemed legit. Tabitha glanced at Phoebe who gave her a thumbs up and whispered, "VFW in Pine Woods."

Tabitha's eyes widened. Pine Woods was in Delaware. They had ended up across the state line. No wonder her feet felt like she'd scoured them with steel wool. Well, softer steel wool since Dennis had wrapped them. She swallowed again then relayed the information to the dispatcher.

"Ma'am, that's all we need. Please hang up."

Hang up? Didn't the dispatchers stay on the line until

the police arrived? The ball of nerves at the base of her spine tingled.

"Hang up? Someone is coming, right?"

A brief pause on the end of the line. "Thank you, ma'am. Police are en route. They will be there in approximately twenty-five minutes. Thank you for calling 911." The dispatcher ended the call.

Tabitha held the phone for a moment, partially stunned, but noticed Phoebe's expectant glare. She handed her the phone back, but she still felt foggy. Not that she had much experience with calling 911, but it wasn't what she had anticipated.

"Everything okay?" Dennis asked, his voice quiet. He pushed his spectacles up his nose.

The sweet, now-familiar gesture soothed her irritated nerves. Her instincts told her she was being foolish. She was hungry and exhausted and worn thin. Of course it was 911. How could the central emergency number have been re-routed?

There was a band on the small stage, dressed almost like a barbershop quartet, and they were still warming up. She focused on the music. It would help, as it always did.

"Yes, the police are on their way. They'll be here in less than half an hour."

"Excellent!" Phoebe clapped her hands. "You guys should definitely join in the party while you wait."

"Oh no, we couldn't." Dennis glanced at the band then at the gathering crowd. "We don't have any money for the entrance fee."

Phoebe frowned and waved a hand in front of her face. "Please, do not worry about it. My treat. You guys have been through enough tonight. Get some food, then join in the dancing. It's a really fun group."

Tabitha's stomach grumbled. She thanked Phoebe, who sashayed away, her polka-dotted petticoats swaying like a bell. "Come on, Dennis, let's get something to eat."

Dennis followed her back to the buffet, and oh heavens, if she salivated any more she would need a comically large bib. She chose a compostable plate, then loaded it with every single thing within her reach. Bratwurst, kraut, potato salad, knishes, a type of goulash, some other unidentifiable thing that smelled like heaven met cheddar cheese and they had a baby. A jolly trim man with a beard that hung halfway down his chest handed her a red plastic cup filled with beer that smelled like wheat fields and limes.

Tabitha returned to her folding chair with her treasure and immediately set to eating. When had she ever been this hungry? After The Incident, she had barely eaten for week. Dennis took the seat beside her, a curious half-smile on his face. Maybe the company helped her appetite.

"What?" she asked through a mouthful of goulash. These dancers could cook. She would definitely hit up the dessert table after she had spoken with the police.

He cut a piece of bratwurst into small pieces with the plastic knife and fork before spearing a cube of it. "I'm glad I finally made it to the restaurant with you."

Tabitha laughed and scooped some salad onto her fork. "Honey, this is absolutely not a date. It is not a date when you are running for your life."

A shy flush crept over his cheeks and he bent toward his full plate. "I don't know. There's good food, music, and a beautiful woman." The flush deepened to a ripe crimson. He hurriedly shoved more food into his mouth and gestured with his plastic knife at the band. "I don't know this kind of music. I like it."

Tabitha still glowed from his description of events. They

were wrong, totally off base, but it was sweet of him to find the positives despite all the horror.

Other guests amassed in the center of the dance floor, splitting into pairs, as the band leader stepped up to the microphone. He cupped the metal head like an ice cream cone.

"Ladies and gentlemen, welcome to the May Polka Party here at the lovely Pine Woods VFW. There is quite the spread of food tonight. Let's have a round of applause for our fabulous potluckers." Tabitha clapped until her palms hurt and whooped like she was at a college football game. "That's right, well deserved. Let's pair up for our dance class, led by the lovely Leah."

Leah, she of the fabulous dress designs, sashayed up to microphone. Her long, straight black hair was tied in a large polka-dot bedazzled bow. Her dress was a mix of denim and gingham with stiff lacy petticoats that swished prettily.

Phoebe moved toward them. "You guys should join in."

Dennis shook his head and looked down at his now-empty plate. "I don't know this dance."

Tabitha held up her hands in the universal gesture of helplessness. There was a lightness in her center, probably from a good meal and pleasant company. "I've never danced the polka, either. It looks like fun."

Phoebe rolled her eyes and grabbed each of them by the hand, hauling them from their seats. "You never know unless you try. Stand next to me and Bill."

9

Dennis pushed his spectacles up the bridge of his nose. His flop sweat made him feel like he was swimming through a thick bowl of goulash. There was too much noise and too many people on this dance floor, too many people who knew what they were doing. Unlike him.

Then Tabitha put her hand on his arm. His world relaxed and the focus narrowed until she was the only thing he saw. Tabitha, with her soft curls hanging loose around her face, the green dress that made him think all sorts of inappropriate things, those bare feet that ran faster and were stronger than any feet had the right to be. In a world of mathematical improbabilities, what were the odds that he would have met the one woman who could make his mind quiet?

He couldn't calculate that now. She had called him 'honey.' That endearment had slipped under his skin, worked itself deep into his blood until it altered his DNA so that he was all of a sudden the sort of man who stood in a crowded ballroom, about to learn a dance to music he had never heard before. The sort of man who ran from danger and survived.

He smiled at her and took her hand as the band began to play.

Up front, the woman in the fancy blue and black poofy dress grinned into the microphone and demonstrated a hand hold with her partner. The band hit a downbeat and an accordion started a tune. He could follow that rhythm. The Dennis who was also 'honey' could count this music. "We're starting you all off easy, folks. The timing is one-two-three-and-one-two-three. Think *oom-pah-pah* and *oom-pah-pah*. Watch Phoebe and Bill first, then join in when you feel ready."

Dennis's heartbeat raced and his palms slicked with sweat. The music was thumpy and boisterous, the direct antithesis to everything he had learned at Anita's ballroom studio. He watched the couple, Phoebe and her friend, making their way around the room, spinning and spinning. He couldn't do this. How had he ever thought he could? He had only ever danced with Anita because she was patient and unthreatening and he wasn't wildly attracted to her.

Tabitha gripped his arm, her excitement palpable. A lump settled in his chest. He was going to disappoint her. "Oh my God, Dennis! It's just like *The King and I!* I can finally live my Mrs. Anna dreams!"

Other couples were starting to move with Phoebe and her friend. Soon Dennis and Tabitha would be run over unless they joined in. "What's *The King and I?*"

Her eyes widened and she slapped at his arm, but in a playful, pleasant way that left a joyous sting on his skin. "You haven't seen it? Deborah Kerr and Yul Brynner? Honey, you are missing out."

And that did it for him. *Honey.* The tiny shifts it created strengthened his resolve and he slipped one hand into hers and the other just underneath her shoulder blade. He grinned, like the Dennis he had always longed to be. "Then let's go."

He whirled around, trying to copy what Phoebe had been doing. It felt awkward, confusing, two left feet and four rights. His brain threatened to shut down his body and stop this complete nonsense. He was a grown man. He shouldn't be making a fool of himself. He was going to run into someone. He was going to—

Tabitha laughed, a clear, crystalline sound that echoed deep within him. She was having fun. Having fun, with him. She was holding him tightly, whirling with him, following him, her eyes wide and bright, her smile stretching toward her ears. Her heat spurred him onward. He tripped once but righted himself and tried to find the rhythm again. One-two-three and one-two-three. *Oom pah pah.*

"You're all doing great, folks." The woman onstage clapped. "If you miss a step, don't worry. Just have fun!"

Fun. That's what this was. Holding Tabitha in this room with these people was fun. Dennis had been wasting his life up until this point. He threw himself into the dance, letting his heart rate rise and quell his anxieties.

The song ended and Dennis whirled one last time with Tabitha. Five more minutes. He would do anything to dance five more minutes with her.

She stopped beside him, her gaze on his face, her hands applauding with everyone else. He should do that, too. Find anything else to do with his hands, when all he really wanted was to hold her again. The loss of her touch felt like dunking his hands in ice water.

She stared at him, her eyes curious, assessing. Did she like what she saw? Dennis never particularly liked what he saw when he looked in the mirror, though he certainly liked his view now. His lungs heaved in his chest, begging, aching with need, need for her and her alone. It had never been this way with Cynthia. How could he have been so foolish as to mistake that casual acceptance as anything close to love?

Tabitha exhaled through pursed lips and pushed her hands over her hair, fixing the strands that had fallen in her face during the evening. He knew he shouldn't. It would be a mistake. But it was as though his fingers moved of their own volition. They caught a wayward strand of her dark curls, and he wrapped it around his finger, feeling its cool, soft sway.

Tabitha's gaze snapped to him. "Do you want to get some fresh air? It's a little warm in here." Almost as an afterthought, she added, "And the police, they should be here soon."

"Right. Sure." He dropped the curl of her hair, his body keening for it, but then she laced her fingers with his. Smiling, she led him outside the building.

10

The night air instantly cooled the beads of sweat on her forehead. What was she thinking?

All right, she knew exactly what she was thinking.

Dennis was nothing like Bryan, nor any of her other serious relationships over her last three decades of dating. They had all been alphas, take charge men who wanted strong women they could bend to their will. Tabitha had never been good at bending, but she had liked the adrenaline rush of the power struggle, the excitement. There was no shame over that. She had been young and had survived a home invasion. Of course she would have been drawn to someone like Bryan.

Bryan would have charged after those home invaders, jumped them, and probably would have gotten hurt in the process. Bryan never would have stood up with her and danced the polka barefoot and disheveled in a room full of people in bespoke dresses. Bryan had never looked at her the way Dennis did, like she was radiant, like she was glorious. Like she was exactly what he had always wanted.

She laced her fingers tighter into his, relishing the way he felt against her skin. Like he fit. Without straining or arguing, he simply fit with her.

"Whew!" She fanned herself with one hand, willing her pulse to slow, willing the calm to flood through her. "Thank you so much. I really enjoyed that." Understatement. Who wouldn't want to live out a cinematic dream with a wonderful guy?

He grinned, the smile making him seem at least four inches taller. "Me too. Do you want to sit down?"

"Sure, Dennis." She settled herself into an aging Adirondack chair on a porch that once had been cherry red. The food, the good company, the dance. All of it combined into a more-comfortable Tabitha. "I don't even know your last name."

He perched on the edge of the chair beside her. "Rayner."

"Dennis Rayner." She closed her eyes and let the name wash through her. It sounded vaguely familiar. "And what do you do, Dennis Rayner?"

"Are we allowed to ask questions now?"

"Sure. Go ahead."

He blushed. "I'm an accountant. I'm pretty sure that's obvious."

"Nothing is obvious, honey. If there is one thing I have learned in this life, it is absolutely never judge a person by their appearance."

He smiled again. When he smiled like that, he definitely embraced the Clark Kent vibe. "I don't need to ask what you do."

"Why not? Didn't we just agree not to judge appearances?"

The smile vanished. He traced a design on the patio with

the toe of his loafers. "It's weird. You'll probably think it's weird."

He needed to stop being so flipping adorable. She placed her hand on his. "I won't think it's weird."

"Okay." He inhaled and exhaled then captured her gaze with his. "I do the accounting for your marketing firm."

"Oh." She took her hand back. "Wait, I thought we had hired the head of DR Accounting—*oh.*" How had she not known this? She had wanted the best, and his was definitely the most trusted accounting firm in the city, but she never dealt with them directly.

Dennis pushed his spectacles up his nose. "I'm sorry. It is weird. I'm not very good with names, so I didn't fully connect the dots until this evening. I really am sorry."

Tabitha said nothing, but steeled her spine, waiting. She knew by now what to expect. The casual rejection, the veiled putdown, the mutual rapid loss of interest in the other as a potential partner. It was all right. The marketing firm she had built from the ground up was her baby, her legacy. Bryan had tried to put her down plenty of times, but she hadn't needed him. She didn't need any man's approval.

Maybe Dennis and Bryan weren't so different. It wasn't her fault she hoped. It was theirs that they were too narrow-minded in their misogyny not to appreciate her hard work.

"It's really admirable, what you've built," he said.

She bristled. "Really. Why is that?" Because she was a woman. Because she hadn't gone to the Ivy League. She had heard it all by this point. It was all bullshit toxic masculinity.

"Because you built something real and you manage it well and you provide people with something of value. I can tell how much you love it. It's rare to see someone so truly dedicated. It's not the same, but I feel like that, too, sometimes. Like my company is my baby." He stared into the dark night. "That probably sounds silly."

It felt like a combination of the floor dropping out from under her feet as well as a rip in the space time continuum. She was speechless for several moments. Someone actually understood? Someone who wasn't in her family, who hadn't seen the sacrifices and hard work? "Wow."

He pushed his spectacles up the bridge of his nose and if she hadn't been completely stunned into stone-like complacency, she would have run her hands over his stubbled jaw and kissed him senseless. Damn sexy spectacles.

"I mean, I work for a lot of companies and see a lot of books. It's amazing to me, as an accountant, what people try to hide and what they don't." He glanced over at her, a pleasant flare in his eyes from the party lights inside the VFW. "No one at your company tries to hide anything. The respect for you is implicit. You do pro bono marketing for youth advocacy nonprofits, which you don't advertise." He traced another picture in the dust on the patio, the toe of his shoe scuffing along the wood. "You do the things I wish I could. I think I liked you even before I met you. I definitely... admire you."

A warmth spread throughout her body, numbing her aching feet, making her feel light and free. "Really? I thought, after you didn't show up at the restaurant, that you had no interest in meeting me."

When he looked up at her, his face was heartbreakingly shy, painfully earnest. This time, the warmth loosened her muscles and she did run a single fingertip along his jaw. His stubble was brushy and soft, the angles of his face clean and sharp. He really was a good-looking guy.

"I'm sorry," he whispered.

"Stop saying that." She leaned toward him, wanting

nothing more than to press her lips to his, to feel that stubble scraping across her cheeks, to feel his heat match her own. This had been a weird night. She might as well have a bit of fun. Even if it wasn't real.

"Tabitha." And dear heavens above, the way he said her name cut straight through her defenses and all of her bullshit. She closed the distance between them, parted her lips, and kissed him softly.

It wasn't a knee-buckling, back-breaking, full tongues-in-each-other's gullet kiss. It wasn't the kind of kiss that preceded some hot and heavy naked play. It was a kiss of promises, a kiss of hope. A kiss between two people who had been around long enough to know that pure fire and passion was always there, waiting just behind this moment, but it got better and lasted longer when there was friendship and respect behind it.

It floored Tabitha, sinking into her bones and settling her in a way she had never before experienced.

They broke the kiss as if by mutual agreement, and she rested her forehead against his. For one moment, she wanted to live in this perfect little bubble.

Dennis Rayner. Who would have thought?

She jostled to awareness of the outside world at the flash of headlights across her cheek and the rustling of a car.

"Thank goodness, the police are finally here." She stood, one arm half-raised in greeting.

"Tabitha," Dennis whispered behind her. One hand encircled her wrist, but his grip was less tender and more icy fear.

Tabitha couldn't move anyway. Shit. What were the odds? The car she had heard wasn't a police cruiser. It was an enormous black SUV with tinted windows.

Her blood froze. Damn it, she knew that 911 call was

suspicious. She had allowed the fatigue and hunger and Dennis to pull her focus. Not any more.

"Run." Tabitha wasn't sure which of them spoke first, as it was nearly simultaneous. She leapt over the Adirondack chair, heading for the rear of the VFW. It was possible it wasn't the intruders and she was overreacting. Possible, not probable. If they were the intruders… She couldn't let them inside, couldn't allow them to hurt these kind people who had done nothing but help.

She and Dennis jumped down the back staircase, the sounds of lively polka music and the scents of bratwurst and stew wafting from the half-opened windows. Maybe they had done it. Maybe they had gotten away just in time.

Her heart galloping, her legs burning, she raced toward the tree line, back toward the forest. They could lose them in the trees, as they had before.

Dennis grabbed her hand and yanked her backward, nearly pulling her off her feet.

She whirled on him. Escape. Focus. She had forgotten to focus and now they were in trouble. Foolish, she had been so foolish. "What are you—"

But then she understood. One man stalked out of the forest, in black tactical gear with their faces masked, a too-large gun cradled in his arms.

She whirled toward the front, but there was another armed man on that side. The home invaders surrounded them. There was nowhere left to turn, nowhere left to hide. She and Dennis had been caught.

The panic roiling within him had no outlet. The gag in his mouth was already damp and cloying. The bindings around his wrists sliced through his skin like a bear trap. The blindfold might have let in outside light were it not for the fact that it was already deeply past his bedtime.

The only small consolation, the one tiny thing keeping him from combusting into an asthmatic hot mess, was that Tabitha was beside him. Tabitha. If there wasn't a gag that smelled like wet dog crammed into his mouth, he would be able to smell her. Or remember how soft her lips were, like kissing velvet.

He had to help Tabitha. He had to get her out of danger.

He tried to shut out the competing sources of sensory overload and focus. That was what Tabitha would do, right? Focus and control. Manage the situation.

He managed his own accounting firm but never gagged, blindfolded, and bound. Never locked in a car with two armed men built like mountains and the most amazing woman he had ever met, the kind of woman who melted his insides like butter on a warm croissant.

Keeping his head down and movements subtle, he shifted toward where he hoped she was. His fingers brushed against hers. There. A slow thrill of warmth coursed through him, giving him strength. He laced his fingers through hers and felt her latch onto him.

He would make them pay. He would not let anything happen to Tabitha.

THE CAR RUMBLED TO A STOP. Not that she could see where she was, with the fucking blindfold. Those bastards had probably messed up her hair, too, the assholes.

She kept her rage close, just below the surface. If she let on too soon, they would see it and punish her. That's what assholes like them did. Fuck them. Fuck all of them.

She heard the card door swing open, and Dennis was roughly ripped away from her. She forced her gagged mouth to protest, but no sounds emerged. A few seconds later, gloved hands grabbed at her shoulders and yanked her from the backseat. She wouldn't make it easy for them, no sir, abso-fucking-lutely not. Not Tabitha Valby. Tabitha Valby, Philly Queenpin, squirmed and writhed and kicked and hit. Tabitha Valby didn't go down without a fight.

One of them struck her, hard, across the face, making her see stars. The pain blossomed along her cheekbone and fired through her scalp, momentarily breaking her concentration. *No. Hell no.*

She registered the hand wrapped around her bicep, forcing her forward, pulling her. She stumbled, and the grip tightened to a vise, lifting her off her feet and practically throwing her. The surface of the ground felt like a threshold, as she tripped and stumbled over the rough fabric of what reminded her of a scratchy welcome mat.

A house. The house? Maybe they were back at the house where this had all started.

Tabitha focused on the pain in her cheek and her arm. She would dive into it, let it open the rage deep inside her, let that anger hone her senses until they were razor sharp.

Escape. Focus. Survive.

The hand on her arm thrust her downward until she knelt on the floor, the cold tile palpable through the thin fabric of her dress.

"Stay there," a gruff baritone said.

Tabitha closed her eyes so she could control the darkness instead of the blindfold. She needed to still her breathing. Thank goodness for those yoga sessions. Initially she had gone for the networking opportunities, but the Ujjayi breathing techniques had several uses.

With her inner voice quiet, she could focus on the external sounds. She heard Dennis's solid breaths beside her and felt the warmth radiating from him. Mentally, she closed the door on his now-familiar sounds and tried to find the other cues. There. Two sets of shoes, one heavy and thumping like a bass drum, the other with a softer, lighter touch. They were moving away from her, farther into the building. She checked for other cues, other sounds, but there were none. The sets of shoes continued to fade, though she felt the reverberations of the heavy steps through the floor beneath her knees.

The intruders were leaving. Idiots. Hadn't they learned not to leave captives unattended?

Their loss. It was time. Escape. Focus. Survive.

Keeping her eyes closed to mitigate the blindfold's effects, she focused on Dennis's presence beside her. She turned her back toward him and reached with her fingertips, feeling along the floor until the pads connected with what she presumed was his thigh. A garbled sound, likely his voice through his own gag, but she didn't have time for that. She tiptoed her fingers along his skin, tracing the lines of his muscles through his pants so she could find his hands. As if he understood what she was looking for, he turned his back to her and their fingers connected again, just as they had in the car. His warmth and steadiness was an anchor, and the unquiet part of her mind eased, allowing her to focus on her task.

She couldn't linger in these sensations. She bent forward at the waist so she could trace her fingers up his back, though she could only go so high with her hands tied behind her. When she reached the limit of her range of motion, she knuckled her fingers into his sweater vest and tugged. It seemed he understood. He slid down the floor until she could grasp the bindings at the nape of his neck. Blind and mute, she used the sensation in her fingers to pull at the knots, to unsnag the fabric holding the gag in place. A rush of triumph coursed through her when she felt it give way.

"Tabitha," he whispered, his voice hoarse and choked. "Let me do you."

She maneuvered into a similar position, and within moments, he had worked her gag free as well. He was pretty flexible, if she were in a position to appreciate that at the moment. "Stay there," he said, his voice barely palpable. Smart man, he too knew the urgency of the situation. She felt the tugging at the back of her blindfold, felt the moment it gave way, and blinked rapidly as she took in her surroundings.

The dim light hurt after so long without it, but she quickly re-accustomed herself to what little there was. She and Dennis sat on a cool tiled floor. It wasn't the same house they had been in before but shared several similarities. Same living room set, same rugs.

Something clicked in her mind. The stagers. It must be the same staging company at both houses. What were they hiding?

"Tabitha," Dennis whispered.

Right. She needed to focus. She turned to the task at hand and within moments, had relieved Dennis of his blindfold. She saw the moment the scant light hit his eyes, the wince and rapid succession of blinks, then the comprehension dawn as he took in the setting.

"We have to go," she mouthed.

She couldn't see or hear the home invaders, but she kept watch. They were sitting in a living room dominated by a red brick fireplace along one wall and a floor-to-ceiling shattered mirror on the other. That was unfortunate. Tabitha winced. Though if anyone deserved seven years bad luck, it was these assholes.

The lights were off, but the exteriors were on, lending a dreamscape-y feeling to the living room, making the shadows dance and curl into menacing shapes. The couch loomed like an ogre and the demonic horns capped either side of the wingchairs.

They needed to get the fuck out of there. She was beginning to hallucinate.

Their wrists were still bound behind them, more

securely this time. She tried bending, contorting herself to move her hands to the front, but after a long night, her muscles did not want to cooperate. She had watched so many videos and gone through so many self-defense courses, and at the moment, it was all for nought.

But Tabitha never gave up. Not when it wasn't just her own life on the line.

Dennis gestured with his head toward the front door. He was right. She was wasting time trying to free herself. It would be faster to escape the house, run to the nearest sympathetic neighbor, and let them cut her free.

She stumbled to her feet and tiptoed behind him to the front door. He moved slowly, as though his leg had been wounded. Where she had been struck, her cheekbone flared with rage and pain. Bastards. Assholes. Ruining a perfectly terrible evening.

Well, bad, then terrible, then awful, then surprisingly fun, and now back to heinous.

Bastards.

Tabitha focused on co-victim. He looked around, assessing, careful, then opened the door so slowly it was as though he were trying to move it through ice. Tabitha held her breath, willing him to go faster while simultaneously knowing that if he did, the hinges could creak, the door could fly open and bang against the wall, anything, anything could happen and then all would be lost.

Once he had it open enough for them to slip through, he turned, and stopped dead in his tracks. Irritation rankled through her, but she tamped it down. There had to be a reason. With Dennis, there was always a reason.

Tabitha turned to follow his gaze, and the fledgling hope she had nurtured hightailed it out of town.

Rita Forest stood in the doorway, a respectably-sized gun held against one hip. She had changed since the gas station, into a blue and gray outfit. The fabric of which rose and fell with the furious pace of her breathing.

Shit. Shit, fuck, damn.

"You two," Rita said.

12

Dennis was not much of one for cursing. Normally he held his tongue, rationalized, did deep breathing exercises.

Not now. Fuck. Fuck, piss, shit, damn.

Rita Forest. Since they had left her behind at the gas station, she had changed into a pair of high-waisted navy-blue pants and a dark gray short-sleeved sweater. She looked like a fucking damned bruise.

He wished he had forgotten her name.

"Colby! Pinter!" she called into the house. They must be the intruders. Last-name-only types. Dennis should have known.

"You two fucked everything up tonight. Sit down." Rita Forest pointed the gun directly at them, and Dennis moved in front of Tabitha. Maybe it was a futile gesture, but she mattered.

His hands still bound behind his back, he reversed until he could feel Tabitha's warmth, just inches from him. As long as she was okay, that was what mattered. He needed to keep going, for her.

"I'm not even going to ask how the two of you got the gags and blindfolds off." Rita kept the gun on them as she followed them deeper into the poorly-lit living room. "But we learned from last time to make the zip ties stronger."

Tabitha yawned audibly. Dennis whirled to silence her, to remind her of the danger she was in, but he caught a gleam of something in her eyes that stilled him. He trusted her. Tabitha knew what she was doing.

"Am I boring you?" Rita clenched her jaw and swung the gun in Tabitha's direction. "Do you know what you've put me through? Trust me, if we hadn't had to go to hell and back to track the pair of you down, I could have been on my flight to Venezuela by now."

"You don't want to go to Venezuela," Dennis said. He felt Tabitha's body shake behind him, almost like she was stifling laughter. "Human rights violations. It's a war zone."

Rita rolled her eyes. "Not if you're rich as fuck, you moron."

"Don't call him that," Tabitha said. "He runs the best accounting firm in southeastern Pennsylvania."

He thrilled a little at Tabitha's praise, but Rita was distinctly unimpressed. "I don't care if he's the richest man alive. Both of you have been giant pains in our ass. I had to call in my contact at the 911 dispatch to find you. I can't burn bridges like that. Colby! Pinter!"

Her voice was getting pitchier. Did that mean she was anxious? Maybe they were getting to her.

"Aww." Tabitha pouted her lips, which was probably the sexiest thing Dennis had ever seen. "Did you lose your henchmen? Millennials these days. You can't treat people like shit any more without repercussions. Have you gotten dissed on social media yet? Had your own #Realtor-BitchBoss?"

Rita's face reddened until she looked nearly purple. She should watch her blood pressure. "Shut. Up."

"Don't say that to her." Dennis hadn't realized he had spoken until Rita glared at him, her eyes full of flint, her face purple. It reminded him of a movie he had seen as a child, something traumatic that ruined chocolate fountains for him forever. "We didn't do anything to you."

"You didn't do anything? The two of you ruined what was a completely wonderful plan."

"A wonderful plan?" Dennis's long dormant ire kindled. In his defense, it had been one impossibly long night. "How was it a wonderful plan to invite people to a fake open house? Why even post it?"

Rita scowled, the lines on her face practically crevasses. "It was a mistake, okay? Like I need validation from *you*. My boss was leaning over my shoulder with his meat breath, asking why the place hadn't sold. So I made a fake open house listing to get him off my back and that idiotic assistant of mine posted it. Fucking amateurs." She shook her head. "I tried to cancel the whole thing, but then you two showed up and overstayed your welcome."

Tabitha yawned again. "So this is the part where you explain your evil genius plan and then say you have to kill us because we've seen too much? Dennis, wake me when it's over."

It was official, he adored Tabitha. Listening to her taunt Rita Forest was the best entertainment he could have imagined.

Rita stamped her foot like a toddler having a tantrum. "Stop it, stop it, stop it!" Tears streamed down her face and she raised the gun again, aiming directly for Tabitha. "I know one way to shut you up for good."

Oh no. There was absolutely no way he would let that

happen. He couldn't let anything happen, not to Tabitha. Now or never. Time to be a hero. Or at least a reasonable facsimile of one. He squeezed his eyes shut, then flung his body in front of Tabitha, shielding her as best as he could with his arms behind his back. She pressed her forehead into his chest, pressed her body to his, and tears welled in his eyes.

If he was going to die, at least he had held her for one more moment.

He froze in that position for one moment, two, every instant knowing the blow would come, the pain would hit, but at least he would have done something noble for a woman who deserved everything good and honorable thing this messed up world had to offer.

But the pain didn't come. He glanced around, searching for Tabitha's eyes, Tabitha's face, but she wasn't looking at him. She was looking past him, her head tilted slightly to the side, alert and assessing. What was going on? He should be dead by now.

Rita Forest stood with her legs splayed and both hands on her hips. She held the gun in her right hand, but it was loose and she kept tapping her finger against the handle. Handle? Dennis knew next to nothing about guns except to run from them as fast as he could.

What was she waiting for? What had distracted her?

"Colby? Pinter?" Rita Forest called.

No answer from the depths of the house.

Her henchmen had deserted her. Not that Dennis would blame them.

There really wasn't any light to speak of in that area. It reminded Dennis of an enormous black shadow monster, lurking and twirling just beyond the fragile moonlight in the living room.

Tabitha nudged him with her elbow. Despite the darkness of the room, he could make out the words she was mouthing. "Get the gun."

That seemed completely obvious, but how on Earth was Dennis going to manage to wrestle the gun from a realtor while he had both hands tied behind his back?

Then, while shaking his head, he saw it. An opportunity. He communicated to Tabitha with his eyes, not even daring to form the soundless words. Her brow furrowed but then comprehension dawned in her eyes and a smile, that would not have been out of place on an Olympic gold medalist, creased her face. Dennis understood. He felt exactly the same way.

TABITHA COVERED for Dennis while he shuffled silently backward toward the fireplace. Stagers, the idiots. How could they have left a fireplace set, right out in the open for any captive to commandeer?

Escape. Focus. Survive with Dennis.

Tabitha stayed still and quiet, as Rita moved further into the dark house. "Colby? Pinter?" Did she not know any more than their last names? No wonder they weren't responding. If Tabitha had been in trouble, her mother would have used her middle, last, and confirmation names, too.

Dennis moved beside her, the whispers of his body echoing through hers. She trusted him to be there, even if she couldn't dwell on the feelings that evoked right now. His frame was slumped slightly forward, bowed by the weight of the iron fireplace poker. He moved with grace, though after his polka, she shouldn't have been surprised. He was an excellent dancer.

She helped him stand, offering her arm for balance. He turned and mouthed the words, "Call her."

Tabitha grinned. "Hey, Rita?"

The realtor spun and approached them, her gait like a herd of thundering hyenas. "What the fuck do you want?" She lifted the gun, but Tabitha could see her aim was way, way off. Uh oh. Someone had forgotten to go to the gun range in her wannabe criminal class. "I am so done with you and all of this sh—"

And that was when Dennis spun around and the haft of the heavy fireplace poker connected with the small of Rita's back. She went flying, the gun arcing high overhead, revolving in the air.

"Shit!" Tabitha watched the arc, as though the pistol rotated in slow motion. She prayed the gun wasn't loaded. If only people could wave around something less lethal.

Rita and the gun hit the ground nearly at the same moment, in near defiance of Newtonian laws. Thank heavens and everything good in the universe there was no burst of gunfire. Tabitha threw her body weight over the gun, the steel greasy from Rita's sweat.

Dennis held the fireplace poker and stood poised over Rita's prone figure, like a freaking superhero on a movie poster. Damn, cinnamon roll heroes were hot.

But Rita was laughing. The bitch had the gall to laugh.

"Colby and Pinter are going to kick your asses," she wheezed, holding the side where Dennis had struck her.

A door creaked open and suddenly a blinding light illuminated the room. She blinked, tightening her hold on the gun behind her back. Shit, what now? She couldn't see anything until her eyes adjusted. Was Dennis okay?

Then a deep voice echoed through the room, drowning out the dying wheeze of Rita's laugh. "I don't think Colby or Pinter will be much help to you here, ma'am. You're all under arrest."

In that same instant, Tabitha's night blindness finally cleared, and her heart leapt.

Holding the two handcuffed home invaders were two of Lewis's finest deputies and Sheriff Forbes. The tall, bald one, who would not have been out of place in a hot Navy officers calendar, was the one who had spoken.

It was over. They were saved. Finally.

Tabitha's grip on the gun loosened, and she heard the solid clunk of the fireplace poker dropping on the hardwood floor.

All eyes in the room converged on Dennis, whose cheeks flared red. "Shit, I'm sorry. That poker's really going to leave a mark in a floor like this."

13

Dennis sat beside Tabitha on the stagers' couch, rubbing his wrists. It had taken an awfully long time, but he was finally getting some of the sensation back. He couldn't help stealing glances at Tabitha from his peripheral vision, but she wasn't paying any attention to him now.

He supposed the scene was pretty dramatic. More interesting than him, certainly.

The two deputies and Sheriff Forbes had called for backup, and the township police had arrived to take Rita Forest and the two black-masked home invaders off to jail. Rita Forest had not stopped spitting and complaining about the pain in her back, and how she was an innocent bystander in all of this.

Dennis wasn't buying that bullshit.

Sheriff Forbes and the tall, handsome deputy approached their couch.

"Hello. I'm Sheriff Forbes, and this is Deputy John Flaherty. We would like to ask you some questions, if you don't mind."

"Of course." Tabitha's smile was weak, not at all her usual one, the one that made him feel like the sun had never really shone until he had met her. "We're happy to help."

He wanted to cover her hand with his, but maybe now that their ordeal was over, she wanted nothing to do with him. He rubbed at the gnawing wound growing in his chest.

Sheriff Forbes had thin wire glasses and a pleasant shock of graying hair. She smiled, and maybe Dennis was delirious after everything that had happened, not to mention eating sketchy polka potato salad, but he felt a little calmer. "So, you two have had quite a night. Could we get your names, please? For the record."

Deputy Flaherty had a tiny spiral notebook that Dennis admired. "Is that a Golden Spiro pen?" he asked. "That's my favorite, too."

"It is," the deputy replied, his smile genuine and warm. Maybe everything would be all right. Tabitha wouldn't talk to him again but at least he wasn't dead. He still had Golden Spiros and forensic genealogy and his office waiting for him on Monday. Even if the thought of it all felt hollower without her by his side.

Still, he was an adult. "I'm Dennis Rayner," he said, sitting up straighter. Posture improved confidence, or so he had read.

"Tabitha Valby."

He really, really liked how she said her name. The pit in his chest widened. Five more minutes with her. That was all he wanted.

"Sheriff Forbes," Tabitha asked. "How did you find us?"

Sheriff Forbes smiled, her eyes soft and patient. "One of your friends, I think from the polka group? She saw the two of you being kidnapped and followed the car. She called us right away, and kept us apprised of your location."

Polka dot Phoebe. "She left without saying anything?"

"We didn't want her to get injured. We let her leave after we arrived."

Tabitha tilted her head to one side. "Didn't you get the 911 call we made?"

Deputy Flaherty and Sheriff Forbes exchanged a look. The sheriff responded. "No. Did the dispatcher give you their name?"

"No." Tabitha tapped one finger repeatedly against her thigh. "I thought it was odd, the call. It wasn't what I had expected. Damn it, I should have listened to my gut. The one time—"

"You couldn't have known." Deputy Flaherty put a hand on Tabitha's arm, calm and soothing. Jealousy flared through Dennis but he tamped it down. Jealousy certainly did not become him.

A single tear appeared at the corner of Tabitha's eye. "So you were here the whole time? The whole time we were held captive?"

The deputy, who shifted his attention to his note taking, lifted his gaze to them. He had kind eyes, deep brown ones that Dennis had a feeling would be helpful in interrogations. "I am sorry we didn't come sooner. We needed to assess the situation, and we weren't sure where they were holding you. We entered through the garage. When the two called Colby and Pinter entered, we took them into custody."

The deputy clicked the end of his pen. "Can you tell us a little bit more about what happened tonight?"

"I don't really know," Tabitha said. "There was a listing for an open house. Dennis was already there when I arrived along with the real estate agent. We wandered around inspecting the house, for, what, fifteen minutes?" She turned to Dennis as if for confirmation. He could only nod. "So, we were getting ready to leave, and Rita, the realtor, went outside for a few minutes. She came back in a little later, all disheveled, and there were two big guys behind her."

"They were dressed all in black." Even he knew it wasn't pertinent, but he wanted to contribute. He had been there with her, and he wanted to hold on to that. "They took our phones and tied us up."

"How did you escape?" Sheriff Forbes tapped the sides of her glasses.

Dennis's breath hitched in his chest and he turned to the woman beside him. "Tabitha. She had watched a bunch of videos online. She figured out how to get the zip ties off. She was brilliant, the whole time."

Tabitha stiffened beside him and cleared her throat. He wished he could wrap an arm around her shoulders. "Dennis found his keys and we managed to get to his car. We didn't know where we were going, we couldn't call anyone. Though I thought at one point I saw Rita texting in the back seat, but she denied it."

"We stopped at a gas station to call the police." He sat up stick straight and his eyes widened. "Oh no, my car is probably still there by the gas pump! Is that dangerous? What if it explodes or something?"

He felt the warm, soft touch of Tabitha's reassuring hand on his thigh, and when he caught her gaze, she smiled. His heart rate sped up at her touch, but even he could read the sorrowful expression in her gaze. This was very, very bad. She wouldn't stay, not with him. Not after they bonded during the trauma. He was going to end up heartbroken in his sad bachelor apartment doctoring store-bought ramen packets with hot sauce.

Tabitha continued. "We tried to get the attendant to call

the police, but the two home invaders showed up instead. We ran. Rita had been in the bathroom, and she tried to grab us as we left. That's when we figured out she must be involved."

"So we walked and walked for a long time. We didn't have any idea where we were. But Tabitha heard music, so we followed it, and that's when we found the polka night." He flushed again. "Please, is there a blanket or something for her? Her legs and feet are all cut up from the forest."

Sheriff Forbes smiled in a patient, assessing way. "We'll get the paramedics to check you out. They'll be here in a minute."

Dennis looked at Tabitha but her gaze was beyond him, on the tall deputy with the spiral-bound notebook. He was standing by the door to the garage, making notations in his book as two other police officers removed cardboard shoe box after cardboard shoe box. They carried them through the living room and into the waiting trunks of the police cruisers. Across the side of one box, in thick black permanent marker, were the words *Disco Balls*.

What the hell?

"Sheriff Forbes?" Tabitha asked. "What happened? Why —why did they do this?"

Dennis watched Tabitha clench her hands together in the folds of her skirt, her knuckles blanching.

Sheriff Forbes stood and stretched her back. "It's an open investigation, obviously. I am very sorry for everything you've been through this evening." She hesitated, her shoulders arching then falling. "We won't know more until we do some investigating, but it looks like they were using the empty homes as warehouses."

He could feel Tabitha's desperation rising off her in

waves. "For what? Rita said the open house listing was a mistake, but what is she hiding?"

Dennis wished he knew what to say to make it better. But he was crap at this kind of thing.

Sheriff Forbes looked apologetic. "I know you want answers. I'm sorry I don't have more for you right now. Why don't you two wait here? The paramedics will check you out, patch you up, and then I'll ask Deputy Flaherty to take you back to your car, and help you gather your things."

TABITHA RUBBED ABSENTLY at the never-ending ache in her chest. She had never sat in a police car before, certainly not in the uber-uncomfortable back seat. The seats reeked of sour ancient vomit and acrid disappointment. Did they think she and Dennis were somehow involved? Maybe that's why the sheriff wouldn't tell them what they had found in the garage. How could they have been involved? Maybe she was just tired and heartsick and her stomach roiled from goulash eaten too many hours before.

It had not taken long for Deputy Flaherty to drive them to the scene of the world's worst open house. Shame, really. Tabitha glanced up at the house, its window shutters open and inviting. It didn't have the feel of a bad place, with Shirley Jackson-style evil. It had not done anything to anyone. A surge of regret coursed through her. If anything had gone right tonight, she could have been putting together an offer for this place.

Now it had been sullied by that bitch and her hulking minions.

She felt Dennis's eyes on her and knew he was watching

every move she made. Well, she couldn't move much from the back seat of the police car. Cold comfort that Deputy Flaherty had rolled the windows down, letting the cool night air cleanse the old-gym-sock sweat from the back seat. She closed her eyes, letting the breeze roll across the dirt and grime on her face. She needed at least eight showers. And a tetanus shot.

The front yard of the open house was lit brightly like one of her photo shoots, apart from the yellow tape and cop chatter. Police and crime scene investigators moved meticulously around the scene, photographing or picking up minuscule pieces of potential evidence with tweezers.

"Did you ever think of doing something like this?" Her voice cracked in her mouth. It felt dry and raw, like she was chewing on leather. She turned to regard Dennis. "Work a crime scene? You said you do forensic genealogy."

She watched his Adam's apple, so prominent in his slender throat, rise and fall. "This is a little too hands on for me." He was, ironically, sitting on said hands, for no particular reason Tabitha could see. "I don't really like blood. I would be so scared of doing something wrong, it would be paralyzing."

"I get that."

"Really? You were amazing. It's like you knew exactly what to do."

A ball formed in her throat. She didn't talk about it. Not any more. She wasn't that Tabitha Valby. She wasn't a victim.

But the story rose within her any way. Maybe it was the stress, the fatigue. Maybe it was because of the way Dennis looked at her. He was a good man. "That's because this isn't the first home invasion I've survived."

She felt his gaze lock on her, but she stared out the window. He didn't say anything. Typical Dennis. Reticent, but present. He covered her hand with his, and with that one simple gesture, the floodgates within her opened.

"I was young. I didn't do anything wrong, though it took me a lot of therapy to realize that." She gulped, but his comforting presence urged her to continue. "Ten years ago, I came home one night to my apartment. An intruder pushed into the vestibule and—and beat me. Robbed me. It hadn't been that late at night. I hadn't been drinking." She couldn't cry over it, not any longer. "My ex, Bryan, he was the officer assigned to my case."

"Oh." Dennis shifted in his seat, his body close to hers but now overpowering. "I see."

She imagined he did. Dennis was like that. Understanding, empathetic.

Bryan had helped her through the entire process, treated her with kindness and respect during that entire six months of hell. Of course she had fallen for him. Of course she had wanted him, had thought it was real love, but it wasn't. At the end of their tumultuous four-year relationship, filled with tears and heartache and blood and sweat, she had vowed never to fall into that pit again. She had taken steps to ensure she would not be a victim again. She took self-defense classes, watched videos on how to escape zip ties, and built up her walls.

What were the odds this would have happened twice in her life?

Dennis squeezed her hand. "You're amazing, Tabitha. You're a survivor. You helped me survive, and I don't know how I can ever repay you."

She couldn't do this any longer. The old trauma burbled beneath the surface of her body, but she couldn't fall into it. Not this time.

The front door opened and Deputy Flaherty ducked as

he emerged, holding Tabitha's purse and Dennis's wallet and phone. An apologetic smile creased his dark brown cheeks, making his eyes crinkle like dried flower petals.

He opened the back seat and handed her the purse. "I need to look through your phones."

Any ounce of energy she may have possessed leached out of her. "Why? We didn't do anything wrong." She glanced at Dennis but he was still sitting on his hands.

"I understand," Deputy Flaherty replied. "It helps to rule you both out as suspects, and we can track your movements and match them to Colby and Pinter. I will bring them back to you tomorrow."

She sighed, every emotion she ever felt weighing her shoulders down as though she were carrying an elephant. "Okay. If you have to, I can manage." Maybe a digital detox wouldn't be awful. Mostly she wanted to go home and sleep.

"That's fine with me, too." Dennis's voice rang hollow with melancholy. Tabitha's heart went out to him. He sounded how she felt.

"Thank you both." Deputy Flaherty slipped their phones into two separate evidence bags then removed his gloves. "Mr. Rayner, I'm afraid your car is still at the gas station, but the police finished checking it and dropped off your key. Do you have your keys, Ms. Valby?"

She fished through her purse but it was more an exercise of disorientation than need. Her keys were where they always were, clipped neatly to the fob attached to the inner pocket. She turned to Dennis. Why was it so difficult to say goodbye to him? They were two people, caught in a shitty situation. Nothing more. Right? She should not have told him about her past. He wouldn't want her now. "I can give you a ride to the gas station, Dennis."

He nodded, shy and stilting.

Her heart lurched as she stepped from the backseat of the cruiser. How long had it been since she had been at the restaurant, waiting for her blind date who hadn't shown? How long had it been since the mouth-watering polka buffet? Since the kiss?

Lifetimes.

Walking the short distance from the cruiser to her car felt more like wading through thick sludge, thick sludge embedded with knives. Adrenaline was an excellent in-the-moment painkiller, but now she could catalog each and every scratch along her lower legs.

She unlocked the door to her sleek silver SUV and pulled herself into the driver seat. Her feet remembered racing through a forest as the pedals scraped her soles. She deserved a large glass of wine and a vat of chocolate frosting.

As she turned the key in the ignition, Dennis climbed into the passenger seat. He fastened his seat belt and sat with his hands stretched wide on his thighs.

The last time they had been in a car together, they had been running for their lives. Hadn't they? Now that the adrenaline rush had ebbed, it all felt like a horrible fading nightmare.

Frustration and anger welled inside her, but she tamped it down, just barely. She couldn't fall apart, not while she was driving. She was Tabitha Valby, queen of control. She pulled onto the street and drove to the corner. A bright red and white stop sign flashed with the reflections of blue and red strobes from the cop cars, mocking her.

"Which way did we go?" Her voice was quieter, scratchier than she had expected, as though it had run a marathon in desert heat and now was suffering from lactic acidosis.

He blinked several times in rapid succession, then turned his head left to right and left again. "Right, I think. South. That line of trees looks familiar."

This was too weird. The easy camaraderie from earlier was gone.

All trees looked familiar when it was pitch dark outside. She glanced at the dashboard clock. Two in the morning. Maybe she would indulge in a rare moment of self-care and go in late to work the next day. Although tomorrow—today?—was Saturday. She sighed in exhausted relief. South sounded as good as anywhere. Dennis hadn't really steered her wrong yet tonight.

She turned right onto the street and drove steadily, willing her eyes to stay open. "Do you mind if I turn on music?"

He shook his head and she pushed the on button for the sound system. Dvorak's "New World Symphony" crept into her bloodstream and soothed every ache. Who knew driving barefoot would hurt so badly after cutting up your feet in a goddamned forest?

"Shit." She hissed and pursed her lips. Hold it together, Tabitha.

She felt Dennis's concerned gaze on her. "What's wrong?"

A hot droplet of moisture wet the inside of her eye. She had to hold it together, if only for a few more minutes.

She sniffed and brushed the tear away with the heel of her hand. "It's nothing."

"It must be something."

If only he weren't so approachable. "I miss my shoes. I know it's silly. They're just shoes and I wouldn't have been able to run in three-inch heels. But I bought them with my first paycheck after opening my agency." She could picture them in the department store, practically gleaming on the little white shelf, drawing in all the light, as if they knew they deserved a spotlight. Peacock blue Mary Jane stilettos. "They were my good luck shoes."

Dennis was quiet for a very long moment. She wondered if she should have apologized, but that thought made her want to cry again. He pitied her, that was it. Now that she had told him about Bryan and The Incident, he pitied her. She couldn't handle that.

"I'm really sorry about your shoes."

"It isn't your fault." They drove in silence for a few moments. Dennis had been right. She remembered this stretch of land, similar shadows and fencing, similar faded, peeling sign advertising FRESH CORN AHEAD LEFT.

He lifted one hand, replaced it, then lifted it again. "Tabitha—"

The shift in the atmosphere was nearly palpable, like Tabitha could reach out and snag it and fold it into an origami dove. "Please don't." Her voice cracked again, brittle and unrefined. This sucked. The whole night sucked. Not knowing exactly what Rita Forest had been up to sucked. Dennis's imminent departure definitely sucked.

She saw the lights of the gas station ahead and flicked her turn signal.

She didn't want to look at him, but in the reflected glow from the station lights, his face was mirrored on her windshield. He looked stricken, broken.

She understood. She felt the same, even if she shouldn't. He was a blind date, her companion in escape. Nothing more. She could not let him be more.

She focused instead on driving, on the routines of pulling into the lot and finding a parking spot. She hadn't focused so hard on finding a parking spot since she was in college and would have done anything to avoid paying downtown Philly prices.

It was better than thinking about Dennis.

She put the SUV in park but left the engine running and gripped the wheel until her knuckles hurt.

"Tabitha?" She couldn't look at him but she heard the aching in his voice. It matched the ache in her heart. It was better to be clean about this, direct. He was a decent person. He deserved the truth. She had been through heartache before. It wasn't worth it.

"This wasn't real." She was surprised her voice was steady, that it was audible at all over Dvorak. She wished in some ways that the music were more maudlin, less uplifting. "None of this was real, Dennis."

"What?" His eyes widened. "Someone attacked us. That was real."

"Yes, of course." She swept hair from her face because she felt as though it would stifle her. "I meant this." She waved her hand once between his chest and hers, the movement making her wrist burn. "Between...us. It's not real."

"I don't think that." His voice was so soft it reminded her of the whisper of a hummingbird's wings. "I like you, Tabitha. I know what I like, and it's you. It's more than what happened tonight."

"It's a trauma bond, that's all. You should go."

He didn't move. She gripped the steering wheel more tightly. "It isn't real, what you're feeling, Dennis."

"What *I'm* feeling? You don't feel it, too?"

Tears collected in her eyes, and she blinked them away. "It isn't real." It hadn't been real with Bryan. With Dennis, it would be pity and fear and misguided emotions. She was too old for this.

"I admire you, Tabitha. I admire the company you built,

yes, but I admire you. You're tough and gorgeous and so smart it makes my brain hurt. I don't believe it isn't real."

A deep pit echoed in her belly, deep in her core. Heaven help her, she wanted to believe it, too. It had been so long since she had felt so drawn to someone, so connected. She remembered the way he lifted her without asking over the prickly tree roots, the way he had held her hand, the feeling of his soft, cool lips against hers. She closed her eyes and breathed deeply.

She had to do this. For both of them. She had been through this before, with Bryan, and look how that had ended. Toxic and bitter and alone. She should stick to her resolutions. Get a dog, buy a house, work. Tabitha Valby, Solo Queen. She had been alone before. It was better that way.

"Please, Dennis. Please go."

He didn't slam the door as he left. He closed it gently, but the soft click reverberated through her mind and heart. She had the sudden, unmistakable sensation that she had lost something forever.

14

Dennis sat in the front seat of his sedan hating himself. He hated that it had taken him an entire weekend to work up the courage to do this. He hated that he hadn't been bold enough when he had the original chance.

It was now or never. Talk to her or spend the rest of his life moping about his failed romantic decisions. Because he knew, now. He knew that what he had felt for Cynthia had never been real. It had never been so deeply a part of him as Tabitha was. She had marked him as indelibly as if she had cut her name into his heart. He had to prove it to her.

He could do this. Now or never.

He went around to the trunk and removed the heavy gift bag and wrapped present. He might have to lug all this up the elevator from the parking garage and lobby to her offices on the nineteenth floor, but he had done difficult things before. Things he had never thought his body or his mind capable of doing, and he had the bruises to prove it.

She was worth it. She was worth everything.

This would be a cakewalk. And if it wasn't, he could go

and drown his sorrows in cake like a respectable failed suitor.

He gave his name and business card to the security desk in the skyscraper lobby and waited patiently for his visitors' badge. The guard eyed the packages warily but said nothing. "Nineteenth floor. Take the East elevators."

Dennis knew that. He had been to her office before, to liaise with her finance department, but he had never been inside her office itself. If he had, if he had met Tabitha before, what might have happened?

He stepped off the elevators and pulled open the polished-glass doorway to her marketing agency.

"Hello, Dennis Rayner from DR Accounting to see Tabitha Valby, please." He was proud he managed to keep the stutter and fear from his voice. The secretary was a petite, rounded woman with her hair held back from her forehead with a gold headband. She checked him through and directed him to wait in the comfortable pale green and blue armchairs in the lobby.

Oh no. All of this planning and Dennis hadn't thought where he would set down his packages. They were too big for his seated lap, and the glass-topped console table with the gilt legs barely looked sturdy enough for the five magazines it already held.

It was ruined. His whole plan was ruined. What on Earth was he going to do?

"Mr. Rayner?" The secretary appeared beside him, her heels barely making any sound. "Right this way. Ms. Valby will see you now."

He gulped his relief and resettled the packages in his arms. He followed the secretary down the hallway toward a large, glass-enclosed corner office.

Of course this would be Tabitha's domain. Professional,

lovely, clean lines and pale colors that reinforced the notion that here was a woman who could do anything well and didn't need anyone else's approval. She honored her own wishes.

If only she wished for him.

"Here we are, Mr. Rayner. Can I get you something to drink?" the secretary asked.

The idea of shortly being in Tabitha's presence thrilled through him. "No, thank you." The secretary nodded and returned to her desk.

Here it was. Here was his moment, his chance. All he had to do was open a door.

TABITHA PLACED a hand to her heart to calm its rapid percussion. Dennis was here? Why? But her secretary, Grace, was never one for pranks, and yes, indeed, standing there in front of her office door was the man himself.

A smile pulled at the corners of her lips. He looked so adorable. He had combed and slicked his hair to the side and was wearing a well-tailored pair of gray houndstooth trousers and a cobalt blue button-down with a white sweater vest. He had dressed up for her.

The racing in her heart sped up a fraction more. Why wasn't he coming in? Of course he could see her, sitting at her desk. That was the entire reason she had a glass-enclosed office, for approachability optics.

Maybe the approximately 300 pounds of gifts he was carrying meant he couldn't get to the door.

Tabitha stood and smoothed the skirt of her wrap dress. She wanted to see him, that was all. They needed to talk. The news that past weekend after the open house from hell had been rife with rumors of drug smuggling, a new designer drug called Disco Balls, "assets" seized from the two properties where she and Dennis had been held. Rita Forrest and her associates arrested and held in township jail as part of a drug ring. Two people needed to discuss something like that, right?

It couldn't be anything else.

Not that she had spent the whole weekend wishing she could talk to him.

She went to the door, feeling a lightness in her shoulders that had been missing since she had stepped into the open house. "Dennis!" His eyes widened and cheeks flushed when she said his name, and something coiled and kindled deep in her core. "It's so good to see you. Please, come in. Let me help you with those packages." She reached for the gift bag and placed it on the floor beside one of the pale yellow chairs opposite her. His movements were stilted. She could see the deep inhale before he entered her office, the hesitation in his steps. But his gaze didn't leave hers. Even as nervous as he was, Tabitha felt like she was the only thing in his field of vision.

She had missed it. She had missed him.

Instead of returning to her own chair across the desk from him, she perched beside him in the other chair. "Please, sit. How are you?"

He sat gingerly in the chair, settling the large wrapped box on his lap. He pushed his spectacles up the bridge of his nose. "Hello," he said after far too long.

Tabitha felt her smile fade. Maybe he hadn't been thinking about her all weekend. And what was with all the presents? Nervousness unleashed her own voice. "How was your weekend? I had the world's longest shower after getting home that night, and I burned the dress I was wearing in effigy." She chuckled though it sounded hollow, even to her own ears. "I spent the rest of the weekend lying on my couch watching the news as my mom called me 800 times to make sure I was okay."

She didn't mention going to the police station on Saturday to pick up her phone. Deputy Flaherty hadn't been there, but Sheriff Forbes had fetched it from evidence. She had told Tabitha they were very lucky to be alive. Along with the seized drugs, oddly called Disco Balls, the police had recovered several cases of assault weapons. In addition to Rita and the fake stagers Colby and Pinter, they had also arrested a 911 dispatcher who had been linked to the gang. Later, she had tried researching the drugs on the internet, but they must be too new as she couldn't even find a half-mention. The sheriff had promised their names wouldn't be released to the public. Whoever had been working with Rita Forest and her henchmen might want retaliation.

She shivered, and that seemed to rouse Dennis.

"Are you cold?" he asked, pushing his spectacles up the bridge of his nose. Damn sexy spectacles.

"No, I'm all right. It was a long weekend." Massive understatement. Though she had felt better after texting her therapist. More grounded. More focused.

"Yes. It was weird, watching the news and knowing that I was there, but I can't say anything."

Yes, exactly. How was she supposed to process the trauma if she couldn't talk about it with her family and friends? There had been only so many ways to reassure her mom, but the woman had the ESP of a true mystic. "I feel the same way." Bryan wouldn't have understood. He would have broken doors and worked too-long hours, ignoring what she needed. Someone there. Someone present. Tears prickled again at the backs of her eyes and she exhaled to keep them at bay. "So, what are you doing here?"

He looked down at the ground, then at the box in his lap. "I—I brought you something. I probably shouldn't have, but the idea occurred to me and wouldn't let me go, and it made me feel like I could at least do something for you."

Warmth blossomed in her chest and her smile returned. Oh, Dennis. There were still decent men in the world. Bryan had done nothing of the sort after her first assault. He had taken her out for coffee and then she had ended up seducing him in the back seat of her car.

In retrospect, she would have rather had a present instead of car-rug burn.

He held the box out for her to take, his fingers brushing hers during the exchange and slow, delicious flames rolled up her arms. "Would you open it now?"

"Hell yes!" she teased. "I love presents." She was a grown-ass woman, though, and her entire office could probably see this whole thing, so she unwrapped the box much more slowly than she otherwise would have done, keeping the paper intact. It was impossible not to smile when unwrapping a beautiful gift.

Pulling the enormous, heavy object from the package, she laughed for the first time since Friday night. "A weighted blanket? Genius."

He flushed again, the reaction so charming she wanted to reach over and run her hands over his clean-shaven cheeks. "You can always return it. I didn't know—I did some research and there was this website that recommended it...I left the gift receipt in the box."

She smiled and shifted slightly, her knees pointing toward him. She could picture him doing research, pushing his spectacles up his nose as he stared intently at a search page. Thoughtful. He was so thoughtful. "I love it. I've always wanted one."

He grinned, the corners of his eyes creasing with pleasure, and handed her the gift bag. "This is for you, too."

"More?" She laughed, a startled, pleased sort of sound. "You're spoiling me."

"It's not enough. It can never be enough. Not for you."

She sifted through the layers of tissue paper and first pulled out a scented candle in a silver filigreed jar. "Sylvan Winds?"

"It smells like the forest. From that night." He shifted again in his seat, folding his hands and latching them in his lap.

She lifted the lid from the jar and sniffed, and he was exactly right. It was the scent of the forest as they had approached the VFW. But it didn't bring back the fear, the discomfort. It reminded her of Dennis, of twirling with him barefoot to polka music, the ring of laughter in the air on a late spring night.

"There's more." He flushed.

She set the candle on the floor beside her and next pulled out a shoe box. Her breath caught in her throat. The tears that she had barely contained all weekend started to flow.

A shoe box. Her size. Trembling, but somehow knowing exactly what she would find because that was just who Dennis was, she lifted the lid. All of the air in her lungs escaped her. Peacock blue Mary Jane stilettos. Exactly like the ones she had been wearing that night, the lucky shoes she had lost.

"I—" She had once known how to form words, hadn't she? "I can't believe you did this. Thank you. Really, this is incredible." No one had ever done anything like this for her.

She was always the problem-solver, the smoother of sharp edges, the planner. She was the one everyone looked to for guidance and the one who projected confidence, the image that she didn't need help. That didn't mean it wasn't wanted at times. That was what Bryan had never understood.

Dennis was different. He saw what she needed, what she wanted, and he understood without trying to make her someone else.

Dennis shimmered in her vision, haloed in her cloud of tears. She wiped them away with the heels of her hands.

He pulled an index card from the pocket of his trousers, adjusted his spectacles, and cleared his throat. "I wrote a speech."

"Of course you did." She smiled. There was nothing she wanted more than to hear what he had to say. She pondered interrupting him, telling him what she was finally realizing, but he had worked so hard. He needed someone to listen to him, too.

He frowned slightly and focused on his card. "Tabitha Valby. From the moment I met you, I remembered your name. And that may not seem unusual, but it is for me. I am not good with names or remembering people, but I could never forget you."

Something flipped and clenched in her chest and she clutched the shoe box to her heart.

"Tabitha, I know that you said it wasn't real, what we felt on Friday night. But I don't believe it. I'm not the kind of guy who falls quickly for someone. I have always had checklists and planners. The moment I met you, everything was chaos and I didn't care. I wanted to know everything about you. I fell hard and fast, and it was weird and uncomfortable, but also entirely wonderful. I think the reason couples who meet in traumatic circumstances don't stay together is because there isn't anything else connecting them. But with you, all I see are connections. All I see is a line between me and you, growing like a tree." He stopped, flushing. "Oh shoot, that was a terrible simile." He swallowed, his Adam's apple bobbing as his forehead reddened. "Shoot, I said 'shoot,' didn't I?"

"No. It's okay." Her voice was choked and her mouth dry despite the tears that wouldn't stop. Thank heavens for waterproof mascara. "It's not a terrible simile. Not at all."

He glanced briefly up at her then down again at his card. He must have written in the smallest font imaginable to get it all on one card. Oh, Dennis. "So, Tabitha, I am here to ask you to give me a chance. A chance to show you that we can have something real. I am not the most exciting man, but I can promise to be there for you and listen to you and support you in whatever you want to do." He paused again and sighed, then looked up from the card and pushed his spectacles up his nose. "That's it. That's all I wrote."

She couldn't look away from him, this sweet, handsome man who brought her lucky shoes and spun her around a crowded dance floor on an otherwise terrible night. Why couldn't she say anything? She wanted to lean in and kiss him. She wanted to make him stay. Every emotion jumbled and warred within her.

Her hesitation had the opposite effect on him. His shoulders slumped. "I'm sorry to waste your time." He spoke so softly she could barely hear him. "I'll go now."

"No, Dennis, wait," she said.

They stood at the same time, Tabitha placing her hand on his arm. He had wonderful forearms—lean, strong, and supple. His were the kind of arms that never strayed during good or bad times. The kind of arms and the kind of caring that endured.

He turned toward her, slow and deliberate.

"Yes," she whispered, but her voice grew with her conviction. This was a good idea. Why had she fought it? She could be both Tabitha Valby, business mogul, and Tabita Valby, girlfriend to a successful accountant/forensic genealogist. This was a new chapter in her life. She didn't need a house, not yet. She needed a person. Someone to take her hypothetical dog for walks with her, someone to go to open houses with, someone to come home to at the end of a long day. There was nothing hypothetical about Dennis.

"Yes, let's do it. Let's make it work."

It was as though he became a different person, like light beamed from every surface of him. "Really?"

She laughed again. "Yes, really. It's just dating. As long as you'll actually show up at the restaurant this time."

"I'll show up." He grinned and took her hand in his, running his thumb over the skin. "Any time, any place. I will be there."

Tabitha stepped into him and wrapped her arms around his neck. He felt warm and strong and just the right type of adventurous for her. He felt like he fit. She molded herself to him and rested her chin against his solid chest. "I'll count on it."

EPILOGUE—ONE MONTH LATER

Dennis tugged at the collar of his blue polo shirt. Tabitha had said she didn't want to go back to the site of their disastrous blind date, but he couldn't help but wonder if this was really a better option. Shouldn't he have tried to be a little more romantic? Found a spot with a good wine-by-the-glass list and soft, subtle music?

Tabitha closed the door of his trusty rust red sedan. He never could get rid of the thing, not now that it had helped them escape from the home invasion.

"Are you sure this is okay?" he asked.

Tabitha tossed her hair, long and curly, over her shoulder. She wore a voluminous bright green and yellow dress nipped in at her waist that reminded him of 1950s sock hops and he loved it. His heart leapt a little, just as it did every time he saw her.

She grinned and nudged him playfully on the arm. "Let me carry the fruit salad." She took the covered dish in one hand and walked toward the doors, her skirts swaying around her legs.

"You're here!" Phoebe called, rushing down the steps of

the Pine Woods VFW toward them. "We are so glad you could come."

"Thank you for having us," Tabitha replied. "We couldn't miss it, not after everything you did for us."

Phoebe put a hand on her hip and tossed her hair. "For you? Don't think I don't know what an anonymous donation means two days after last month's party."

He felt Tabitha's gaze on him and he flushed. What was he supposed to have done? Should he have neglected to repay their kindness? It was only money.

Tabitha chuffed him again on the shoulder, but it was soft, playful, and made him feel as though he could do anything, even return to a polka party in the woods of Delaware.

He couldn't fully believe the last month had happened, that he had been able to spend more time with Tabitha. Nothing had ever been so instantaneously pleasant for him. They brunched on Saturdays, visited dog adoptions on Sundays. Neither had the stomach yet for real estate hunting, but maybe someday. When he came home from a long day at work, he could call her and talk through forensic genealogical cases. They had been through enough to want to take things slowly, but for the first time in his life, Dennis felt like he had found his person.

Which was why he was handing over the fees for their admission to the ticket taker at the door and bouncing on his toes to warm up before the dancing started. Anita had taken some of his regular lesson time to teach him polka moves. He hoped Tabitha would be surprised. He would do anything to impress her, as she impressed him daily.

Tabitha sashayed toward the buffet table, chatting animatedly with Phoebe. The band had started already, playing lively music in the background. Last weekend,

Tabitha had sat next to him on the couch with a bowl of popcorn and a bottle of sparkling wine and they had watched *The King and I*. Dennis wouldn't say it was his favorite movie, as nothing could ever top the true classics, *War Games* and *The Wizard*. But he would not have traded watching it with Tabitha for anything, especially after she promised him an '80s movie marathon tomorrow.

She turned her head and smiled broadly at him, joy clearly visible on her face. Love. He loved her, so desperately. One day soon he would tell her. He would tell her how she changed his life, how she changed him. How he was a better version of himself with her, and he would spend the rest of his life treating her like the goddess she was.

He just had to get through this polka first.

Phoebe bounced up on the stage and commandeered the microphone. "All right, everyone! Let's get this shindig started! Grab yourself a partner and have fun!"

Dennis took Tabitha's hand and led her onto the dance floor.

Oom pah pah.

DID you enjoy Tabitha and Dennis's story? They had their start in *Ballroom Blitz*, a fun, fast-paced dance romance suspense with a lot more ballroom dancing. You can get Ballroom Blitz from all major online retailers.

AFTERWORD

Thank you for reading!

Please rate and review, I cannot tell you how much it helps!
If you like this, please sign up for my mailing list to have access to free extras, free books, and lots more.

ACKNOWLEDGMENTS

Thank you so much to my editor and my beta readers, who really helped shape and improve this story.

And thank you to my family, who is always supportive, even when Mom can't play because she's writing. Love you!

ABOUT THE AUTHOR

Love is an adventure.

Natalie writes romances and cozy mysteries featuring women who want to be seen and the men and women who cannot look away from them.

Natalie lives in Los Angeles, where writing is an acceptable way to avoid sunburn. She is mom to two lovely young munchkins who despise brushing their hair and eat way too much cake. She is unapologetically terrible at taking selfies. For updates on new releases and more, check out Natalie Cross Writes